Violet Hunt

The Maiden's Progress

Violet Hunt

The Maiden's Progress

ISBN/EAN: 9783337026509

Printed in Europe, USA, Canada, Australia, Japan

Cover: Foto ©Andreas Hilbeck / pixelio.de

More available books at **www.hansebooks.com**

THE

MAIDEN'S PROGRESS

A Novel in Dialogue

BY

VIOLET HUNT

LONDON

OSGOOD, McILVAINE & CO.

45 ALBEMARLE STREET

1894

I BEG to thank the editors of *The Sketch* and the *Pall Mall Gazette* for permission to reprint several of the chapters of this novel which have previously appeared in their papers.

V. H.

I

A GIRL'S bedroom in a house in Queen's Gate. MARY ELIZABETH MASKELYNE, afterwards known as MODERNA, eighteen, lying on the bed in a white peignoir. Enter on tiptoe her sisters VERONA and PEGGY, aged seventeen and fifteen respectively.

MODERNA, sleepily, raising her head.

What is it? Is my dress come? What time is it?

PEGGY.

Sh-h! There, you *were* asleep, though you said nothing should induce you! It's five o'clock, and I've asked Minching, and there's not a sign of it!

MODERNA, with tragic emphasis.

I simply can't go if it does not come.

PEGGY.

Oh, I daresay it's all right. Mrs. Young never fails. Besides, you could wear your white, or your pink, or...

MODERNA, contemptuously.

The same as you've both got one of! Don't you see that this is a "come out" dress? It's quite different.

B

PEGGY.

Yes, I know—got a train, and a waist, and "decollted"!
(Drawing her breath between her teeth.) Oh, dear! I know you
won't be our "pal" any more.

MODERNA, seizing a foot of each as they lie on her bed.

Oh, yes, I shall, girls; I shall, really! I shan't go
away from you a bit. You know it will be ever so much
nicer for you both when you come out, for I shall be
able to advise you, and tell you things.

PEGGY.

Good gracious, what a plague you will be! I sincerely
hope you will be married off before *I* come on, or I
shall have no peace.

VERONA, thoughtfully.

But, I say, doesn't it seem absurd that *coming out*
should make such a difference! Here are you, you are
only a year older than me, and I am taller—but (hastily) I
don't want to fight!—just a girl like anybody else, and
to-morrow—! To-morrow you will be "grown up";
you'll sit in the drawing-room and leave off lessons—
you're in the middle of the *siecle de Louis Quatorze*
now, I envy you getting out of that — you'll forget
how to turn somersaults; you'll neglect your dormice,
and leave your birds to Peggy and me; and have
secrets with mother, and just be a horrid grown-up
woman like the people that come on mother's reception
days. A woman! Hateful!

PEGGY, sententiously.

I read in a book the other day that a woman was an infernal machine.

BOTH THE OTHERS.

What do you mean? Where?

PEGGY.

Study, second shelf from top, near the door. Such a funny book, all about Woman with a capital W!

MODERNA.

It was Carlyle, you idiot!

PEGGY.

Not at all. It wasn't history. Shall I see if I can remember any of it? "These delicate creatures, as dangerous as a smiling sea, as wavering as the winds, as subtle as fire. . . . In their smiles lurk unknown potentialities of destruction and death. . . . Their frown may wreck empires. . . ." I forget the rest.

MODERNA, pensively.

Is one all that, I wonder?

PEGGY.

You! I don't call *you* a woman! You look about ten!

MODERNA, piteously.

Oh, girls, do I really look so awfully young? It's too bad. Putting me to bed like this is the worst thing possible. If I were tired I should look much older.

PEGGY.

Well, but you are not resting much.   Lie still, old girl, and don't wriggle so.

MODERNA.

Considering that you are both sitting on my foot. . . . Do you know, I don't think men mind our looking young, much—that is, if they are rather old themselves?

PEGGY.

And if they are very young, they snub *us*.   Look at Billy Danvers, he never will talk to anybody but Mrs. Mortimer.   I don't suppose he will give you more than a couple of dances to-night at Aunt Riddell's, Moderna.

VERONA.

Who cares for Billy?   There will be new people. Promise, dear, promise faithfully to tell us all the compliments you get.   Every one!

MODERNA.

All I can remember. (Hastily.)   If there *are* any, I mean.

PEGGY.

I wonder who you'll dance with?   Perhaps you'll meet your Fate?

VERONA, pensively.

The "Unknown God."   Father says every young girl raises altars to the "Unknown God."   I wonder . . .

PEGGY.

If Moderna finds a god to-night, I shall think it very silly of her. As if she wanted to get engaged straight off! She ought to have some fun first. Besides, you know, Aunt Riddell's people are all so dull and political; I'm sure the 'Unknown God' won't be there.

VERONA.

Billy is going, and Mrs. Mortimer, and Mr. Darcy, and the Rensselaers, and Edward—

PEGGY.

Ah, but he isn't going till late, he told me so, he's going to finish the Index. Papa wants it done in a hurry.

MODERNA.

You seem to be always in the study, Peggy. I am sure you must bother Edward dreadfully.

PEGGY.

Not at all! It is a mutual aid society. He helps me with my French exercises, and I cut his pencils for him. Besides, he's Father's secretary and a sort of relation; and it is his business to be useful to me. Father pays him!

MODERNA.

Silly, he doesn't care for the pay; he's rich; he comes because he likes grubbing at Ancient Britons with Father.

I prefer modern ones. (Meditatively.) I shan't bother with
Edward much.   I can see him here every day.

PEGGY.

I like Edward, I must say.

MODERNA.

All children do . . . (Before PEGGY can resent this, Mrs. MINCHING
enters with a dress box. She nearly drops it.)

MRS. MINCHING.

Miss, your dress has come.   Miss Peggy and Miss
Verona, what are you doing in here?   Orders was, that
your sister was not to be disturbed, and Miss Peggy,
your boots on the nice clean counterpane!   I'm sure I
never knew you was here.

PEGGY.

We didn't mean you to, Minching.   Here, let us see!
(They take out a white ball dress, trimmed with lilies of the valley.)
.

MRS. MINCHING, critically.

Very young, and *very* pretty!

MODERNA.

Minching, you are simply sickening with your "young."
Let me see if it fits.   (Assumes the dress in feverish haste.)

PEGGY, her head on one side.

Anything would fit you.   You're as straight as a board.
(Critically.)   Well, I don't much mind it. . . .

VERONA.

Yes, I like those bows on the shoulder. Mind you don't bite them off, dear.

PEGGY.

What has she made your waist?

MODERNA, with dignity.

What it is.

PEGGY.

Oh, nonsense, I know better than that; waists are made, not born. I shall soon begin mine. At present I prefer to be comfortable.

MODERNA.

You haven't laced this properly, Minching. Look what a gap there is!

MRS. MINCHING.

What's the good, Miss; you're only trying it on.

MODERNA.

I forgot. (Impatiently.) Well, will it do?

PEGGY.

Yes, you look rather yellow, but the dress is lovely. Sarah Fullerton Monteith Young has surpassed herself. She looks almost grown up, doesn't she, Aurélie? (To Mrs. MASKELYNE's maid, who enters.) What have you got there?

AURÉLIE.

Mademoiselle, un bouquet! (Holds up her hands.) Ciel! que c'est jeune, que c'est simple! C'est l'innocence même!

PEGGY, with contempt.

Who's innocent? . . . What are you doing, Moderna?

MODERNA, seizing a hairpin, blackening it in the flame of the candle,
and applying it to the corners of her eyes.

Perhaps a few wrinkles would make me look older.

PEGGY.

You will only look as if you had a dirty face.   Don't
be a fool, and tell us who the bouquet is from?

MODERNA, examining the card.

Pooh !   Only Edward !

PEGGY.

Now who else do you think it *could* be from?   Edward
is the only man you know—as yet.

MODERNA, closing her eyes dreamily as the dress is put aside.

As yet ! . . . .

II

IT is three o'clock in the morning.   There is a light burning in
MODERNA'S room.   She enters, flinging off her cloak.   She is un-
laced in silence by Mrs. MINCHING.

MODERNA.

There, Minching, you can go.   Good-night !   I don't
like that dress at all.   It's far too high in the neck and

too short in the train—mother chose it—and there is
quite a new way of doing the hair. You must learn it.
Good-night ! (Exit Mrs. MINCHING.) Dear me, my fan's
broken, the one Aunt Eliza gave me. It's very handsome, but it's not at all the fan for a girl. (Undoes her hair.)
Poor old Minching ! She really doesn't do for a fashionable maid, and mother keeps Aurélie all to herself. We
ought to change. Oh dear, I'm not a bit tired. I could
go to another ball straight off. (The door of the wardrobe opens
and VERONA comes out in her nightgown, while PEGGY creeps from under the bed.)

VERONA.

Well ?

PEGGY.

Well ?

BOTH AT ONCE.

Was it nice ? Who did you dance with ? Are you
engaged ? Did you get many compliments ?

MODERNA.

Not to my face, child.

PEGGY.

Oh, she's going to call us child now ! (Wrapping herself in an
opera cloak with pink ostrich feathers, and squatting on the floor.) Now let
us be comfortable. How scratchy these feathers are !
What sort of ices had you ?

MODERNA.

Do you really suppose I noticed ?

VERONA.

You generally do more than notice. Did Cecilia Riddell wear her little brass heart like mine? She promised me she would.

MODERNA.

What babies you both are!

PEGGY, resigned.

Yes, I knew she would go on like this. Well, Miss Come-outer, tell us all about yourself. Did you meet HIM?

VERONA.

The " Unknown God?"

MODERNA.

I'm so tired of all that! I hate things out of the classics; they're so old-fashioned.

PEGGY.

Yes, father is tiresome. I don't understand what he's talking about, half the time, but I pretend to. It's better than crying, like Verona.

VERONA.

I hate having quotations squirted at me. I get enough of it at school. Father would try the patience of a saint, let alone a schoolgirl. How did they behave, by the way?

MODERNA.

Moderately well. Mother kept smiling at me all across the ballroom, and father actually asked me in a loud voice if I was enjoying myself!

VERONA.

And weren't you?

MODERNA.

Oh, yes—pretty well—but he needn't have asked me before everybody. I'll have to teach him. . . .

PEGGY.

Gracious! She's going to teach father now! We shall see what we shall see. (Wrapping the cloak about her.) Well, I wish you would give a civil answer to a civil question. Who *did* you dance with? Any of *my* friends?

MODERNA.

Who are your friends? I danced with, let me see— (counting on her fingers) one—Mr. Deverel—

PEGGY.

I know him. Towzer bit his leg once, as he was coming in here. He was a brick, he never told. How often with him?

MODERNA.

Twice. Mr. Darcy twice—

PEGGY.

I know him too—through the bannisters. Go on, who else?

MODERNA.

Mr. Danvers.

PEGGY.

Mr. Danvers! Billy! Oh, he doesn't count. He's only just out, like yourself. Go on.

MODERNA.

Mr. Gontram Vere, he's a poet ; he's going to dedicate
one to me !   Then there was Mr. Smudg'em, the R.A.,
he wants to paint me—as an angel—

PEGGY, sarcastic.

Did you say an angel ?

MODERNA.

He says I've got a Botticelli profile . . . Mr. Vere says
I'm like a Romney—

PEGGY.

You will be so conceited there will be no bearing you.
Verona and I will have to keep you down.   Well, go on,
who did you dance *most* with ?   (Searchingly.)

MODERNA.

Well, let me see—it must have been Edward, I fancy.

PEGGY.

You said you weren't going to bother about Edward !

MODERNA.

I know, but—our steps go well together—and—

VERONA.

And who did you go in to supper with ?

MODERNA.

Edward.

VERONA.

And who put you into the carriage?

MODERNA.

Edward.

PEGGY.

Why, it seems all Edward.   ·

MODERNA, angrily.

It wasn't my fault—he seemed to be there somehow.

VERONA.

I like Edward. (Yawns.) What a funny blue shade on that curtain. I never saw it before.

MODERNA.

That's the dawn, silly.

PEGGY.

How can they call it "rosy fingered," then? It's most dreadfully cold and unbecoming. It makes you both look quite green, especially Moderna.

MODERNA.   .

Look here, I hate being stared at. You had better go to bed, both of you. It's four o'clock.

PEGGY.

Ah, now you're getting fractious. Little girls ought not to sit up so late. (Politely.) We won't keep you. Goodnight.

VERONA.

I can go back and lie down, but I am sure I can't sleep any more now, the birds are beginning to make such a racket. Good-night. (They retire on tiptoe.)

MODERNA'S DIARY.

April 29th. My first ball. It is 4 A.M. Minching and Peggy and Verona have just left me. I must try and recall the events of the evening. I had a white dress trimmed with lilies of the valley—rather pretty. Cecilia Riddell had daisies. Aunt Riddell had diamonds. What waste! I danced twenty-one times— twice with the son of the house. I danced three times with a Mr. Donkin. I can't remember whether it was twice or three times with Mr. Deverel. I danced the Lancers with Edward; and I went in to supper once with Mr. Vere and once with Edward. That is all I can remember. I was decidedly nervous at first. I don't think people thought me pretty — there were such lots of awfully pretty girls there. They seemed to know everybody so well, and they all looked older than I. I look too dreadfully young. Cissy Riddell looked a perfect infant in her rational Liberty frock, that's one consolation. Mrs. Mortimer was kind. She said, "Who did your hair, child?" and gave it three pats that quite altered it. She's only twenty-seven and her husband's an M.P. She snubs Billy as I snub Edward. Edward said—

April 30th. What did Edward say? I must have fallen asleep just there. I have just come back from the theatre. We saw Calder Marston as Ingomar. I never saw anything so splendid in my life. He is a great actor. I can't forget his face, nor can Cecilia. I like plays better than balls. I could go every night for a year to see him. . . .

III

MRS. MASKELYNE's drawing-room. MODERNA seated at the tea table with her cousin CECILIA RIDDELL. Mrs. MASKELYNE and Lady RIDDELL in another part of the room. Callers—conversation —tea.

CECILIA, to MODERNA, in a low voice.

Well, dear, and how are you after last night?

MODERNA.

Oh, darling, you know how I feel! I think I like him best in this part. Wasn't it divine? Wasn't it splendid? His eyes—wait—I must take mother some more tea. (Coming back.) Cecilia, dear, did you notice—I am sure it was accidental—how his foot slipped in the third act just as he was going to kneel? What a funny little laugh he gave. Quite a drawing-room laugh, wasn't it?

CECILIA.

Of *course* I noticed. Oh, how sweet he must be off the stage !

MODERNA.

Did I tell you? I met a girl who knows him at home

Her mother's uncle is his god-father.   I have made
great friends with her.   She's perfectly hideous.

CECILIA.

And last night I met a man who could imitate him, and
I shut my eyes and fancied it was Ingomar.   I made
mother ask him to dinner.

MODERNA.

Oh, ask me !

CECILIA.

Of course, darling.   Did you see that notice of him in
The Blowfly ?   I *was* angry.   It said—no, I *won't* re-
peat it.   Some one who had a personal spite against him,
I should say.

MODERNA.

Jealousy, dear, of course.

    *   *   *   *

MRS. MASKELYNE.

What *has* Moderna put in my tea ?   It's perfectly
abominable !

LADY RIDDELL, laughing.

Sprinkled it with salt instead of the muffin, I should
say.   What can you expect of a girl with the Calder-
Marston fever ?

MRS. MASKELYNE.

Don't laugh, Anne, I feel very anxious about it.   I am
obliged to go away for a week, and I have asked her
Aunt Eliza to come and stay here and look after
Moderna.   I am so afraid of her taking some mad,
unusual step. . . .

LADY RIDDELL, smiling.

I don't fancy Eliza would be able to prevent Moderna
taking any step she chose. You have spoilt the child
so. But still there is not the least occasion for anxiety.
It's one of the girlish diseases. Works itself out. Treat
with tolerance and occasional visits to the theatre, and
counter-irritants in the shape of desirable young men,
and disillusionment very soon sets in. I know five
patients at this very moment.

MRS. MASKELYNE.

I know it's very common. But Moderna knows all his
plays by heart, and plagues the other children's lives out
with making them give her her cues, at all times and
seasons. She's quite capable of refusing a good offer
for his sake—for the sake of a wretched actor !

LADY RIDDELL.

My ridiculous girl is just the same. She wears one of
his photographs as Caliban next her heart. Spoils her
figure, that's all I say. Never interfere with girls.
Laugh at them, that's my plan. Cecilia is going to
Girton. That will cure her.

MRS. MASKELYNE.

I believe my daughter has forty-nine photographs of
him in her room.

LADY RIDDELL.

And the fiftieth under her pillow, I expect. Treat for
the housemaids ! Who is this long-haired idiot coming

C

in, with his mouth open, and his eyes shooting out of his head ?   Cupid gone to seed.   Deplorable !

MRS. MASKELYNE.

Sh-sh !   He'll hear.

LADY RIDDELL.

'Always say what I think.   What does he do ?

MRS. MASKELYNE.

Mr. Gontram Vere.   I'm afraid he writes poetry. Moderna met him at your house.

LADY RIDDELL.

Somebody brought him, then.   I don't know him. 'Seems very intimate.

MRS. MASKELYNE.

Quite harmless, I assure you.   He often comes here, but she laughs at him.

GONTRAM VERE and Lord CONISTON and two ladies go up to Mrs. MASKELYNE and shake hands.   Lord CONISTON walks up to the tea-table.

MODERNA, offering him tea.

Two lumps ?   (Aside.)   Why did you come ?

CONISTON, to MODERNA.

One, please.   (Aside.)   I had to go on coming, so I didn't see the use of leaving off.

MODERNA.

Oh, very well, if *you* don't mind.   Would you let me introduce you to those two ladies over there ?   I want to throw a man to them. (Introduces him and resumes her conversation with her cousin.) Cecilia, listen! Flossie Rensselaer confessed to me that she went to the stage-door once, with a huge bouquet of roses to give him. And then when he came out she turned frightened, and daren't give them; but she heard him say, "Home, Wilks," to the coachman. His name's Wilks, you see.

CECILIA.

I wish I was Wilks. I should like to be his servant, his page, and never marry any one.

MODERNA.

Of course not, dear, nor will I. I must tell you something. A man asked me to marry him last night.

CECILIA. ·

Oh, Moderna, how ni— I mean, how dreadful! Who? And how did he— ?

MODERNA.

Only Edward. You know, his uncle died a month ago, and he's Lord Coniston now, and he's going abroad . . . and so he thought . . . that I . . . anyhow he proposed. . . .

CECILIA.

Tell me the very words.

MODERNA.

He said, "I want to ask you something"; and I said, "What?" and he said, "The usual thing"; and I said, "It can't be."

CECILIA.

Dear, you should have pretended not to understand.

MODERNA.

But I did—he was so—

CECILIA, eagerly.

Pale?   Ghastly?

MODERNA.

No, red—and then I said, "Forgive me."

CECILIA.

What for?

MODERNA.

For—for refusing him, I suppose; and then he said, "Some one else?" and I nodded.

CECILIA, horrified.

You didn't say *who*, I hope!

MODERNA.

Oh no, why should I compromise HIM?   Bother! Here's Mr. Vere coming.   We will have to talk to him.

GONTRAM VERE, to MODERNA, pompously.

Miss Maskelyne, I have brought you a little offering.
(Produces a long, thin, green volume.   She takes it and examines it.)

MODERNA.

To Moderna inside!   How nicely you print!   And how funny of you it is to always call me that!

GONTRAM VERE.

Moderna, or Madam Nowadays. It suits you. Haven't you noticed how every one has adopted the name that I christened you with at your first ball? I'm sure your people call you Moderna, now.

MODERNA.

They do. Everybody does.

GONTRAM VERE.

Because it fits you exactly. You are so intensely, essentially modern. You are of the times, you will grow with the times, you will take the impress of every passing wave of modern thought and yet preserve your individuality. You will never stop growing till you die, like me. You have evolution in you, you know. So few women have. Oh yes, I can read you like a book. Some day you will remember this little conversation, and my prophecy. Shall I read the little poem I have written to you—*To Moderna ?*

MODERNA.

Oh no, please, it would make me so dreadfully nervous. I will read it to myself to-night.

GONTRAM VERE.

Ah, you must not take it too seriously. A small volume of Poems, and a large stock of cynicism is as necessary to the equipment of a man of the world as a visiting card. He must be able to dance, make epigrams at call, to write a sonnet—

CECILIA.

I hate sonnets, I always think they are like bricks.

GONTRAM VERE, sternly disregarding her.

Sonnets thrown off, as it were, in the unconsidered moments of this worldly life one leads—that one cannot help leading—lines written between two calls on two of the prettiest women in London, or while I am tying my white tie to go and dine with another. You must read it in the spirit in which it was written.

MODERNA, aside.

I will read it while I am lacing my boots. (Aloud.) Thank you so much. Why is it—excuse me—dog-eared?

GONTRAM VERE.

Symbolical ! I tried to choose a binding that should suggest the inconclusiveness of it all ; something crude, inchoate, ragged, like the thoughts inside—the long, vague, far-reaching, infinitely touching thoughts of a young man. There is nothing final, nothing set about these verses of mine ; they are the early blossoms of a poet's garden, pale, blemished petals, blown this way and that by the early winds that sweep across and ravage it—tokens, signs of the stormy April of life, the "confusions of a wasted youth." You know Swinburne's magnificent lines—

> " Earth is not spoilt for a single shower,
>   But the rain has ruined the ungrown corn."

I have called the volume *Green Thoughts*, you see.

It was written, most of it, on a reading tour in the New Forest—a party of beautiful boys—I myself—

CECILIA, severely.

I thought you said just now you lived on Chelsea Embankment?

GONTRAM VERE.

Ah—oh—*you* see the idea, Miss Maskelyne?

CECILIA, irrepressibly.

I've read " Mr. Verdant Green at Oxford." Is it that sort of thing in poetry?

GONTRAM VERE.

My *dear* Miss Riddell! Is it possible you don't know Marvell's exquisite lines— ?

> " Annihilating all that's made
> To a green thought in a green shade."

Think of it! Green, translucent, quivering leaves—

MODERNA.

Take a back seat, Cecilia. (To Coniston.) More tea.

CONISTON.

No, thank you. I'm off.

MODERNA.

Where to?

CONISTON.

Japan.   .

MODERNA, sharply.

What nonsense!

GONTRAM VERE, languidly.

Why not Birmingham? It's just as dull.

CONISTON.

Very likely—but not so far.

Shakes hands all round and exit.

GONTRAM VERE, shaking his head.

Ah, poor fellow! He is in a very parlous state. . . .

CECILIA, laughing.

What do you mean?

GONTRAM VERE.

That nervous terseness of expression, that insane desire for complete social occultation, in a person so rightly balanced as Coniston—I admire his rationalism, though nothing would induce me to emulate it—can point only to one common form of aberration. He is in love!

CECILIA, severely.

Well, Mr. Vere, don't you believe in love?

GONTRAM VERE.

Hardly. I am a poet.

CECILIA, stoutly.

I believe in it, don't you, Moderna?

GONTRAM VERE.

Really, do you know, Miss Riddell, I think your ex
cellent mother has not brought you up properly.

CECILIA, giggling.

Oh, do go on.   You are so funny.

GONTRAM VERE.

This is your first season, I believe.   You ought still to
be very cynical.   Years hence you will grow your first
illusion.   For a brief period it will suffice you, you will
be foolishly, idiotically happy, then—

CECILIA.

What ?

GONTRAM VERE, sadly.

Illusions, like wisdom teeth, are last to come and first
to go.

CECILIA.

I think you are horribly cynical, Mr. Vere.

GONTRAM VERE, delighted.

Am I ?   But you, dear Miss Riddell, are really a most
curious anachronism.   You have begun at the wrong
end of life.   (His head on one side.)   So young, and yet so
innocent !   .

CECILIA.

I don't care.   I know there is such a thing as true
love nowadays, isn't there, Moderna ?   (Exchanging glances.
The love that asks nothing, expects nothing, is content
with merely the thought of—(Blushes ; so does MODERNA.)

MODERNA.

You see, I am not so up-to-date as you think, Mr. Vere.

GONTRAM VERE.

You are so up-to-date that you have learnt the value of pose—like a true woman. The "Cynthia of the minute" knows what rainbow cloud suits her best.

CECILIA.

Always affected, always unnatural, are we? You have a low opinion of us, Mr. Vere.

GONTRAM VERE, sighing.

Yes, I wish I were not so cynical about women.

MODERNA.

One pose is as good as another. The "modish Cupid of the hour"—how does it go on? This is in exchange for your Cynthia.

GONTRAM VERE, aside.

Sharp little girl! (Aloud.) May I hope for your opinion on my poor verses, dear Madam Nowadays? (Rising.)

MODERNA.

I will write them. Thank you so much for giving me the book, Mr. Vere. *Ungrown Corn*—no, *Confusions*—what is it?

GONTRAM VERE.

I shall be proud if you will rename it. Good-bye!

Exit.

MODERNA.

I think I shall write *my* book, Cecilia. I've wasted my youth too. What shall I call it? *The disused Pea-shooter*, or *Paper Pellets of the Past?*

CECILIA.

If he were to guess we were laughing at him?

MODERNA.

He would never guess, unless we were to tell him. He must never know. It would kill him. I am glad I remembered that quotation. I wasn't going to be out-done. I say, do take your mother away. We are going to "The Tragedy of Laughter" to-night—so are you, aren't you?—and I like to be very, very early for Calder-Marston.

IV

IT is the morning of the Eton and Harrow match. WILLIAM HENRY GERVAISE MASKELYNE, sixteen—middle division at Eton—in the boats—is working an amateur form of heliograph with his cousin RIDDELL, minor, in the house opposite. He has chosen his aunt's bedroom as most convenient for the purpose. Enter his sister hastily, with a tear in each eye.

MODERNA.

William !

WILLIAM, with his mouth full of string.

Oh, blow, what do you want?

MODERNA, breathlessly.

Look here, William. Is it not too mean and unfair?

The Rensselaers promised to call for me to-day to take me to the match, and now, would you believe it, Aunt Eliza says I'm not to go? Tiresome, interfering old thing! If I had known it was going to be like this, I'd never have let mother go away and leave her to manage me!

WILLIAM.

Not to go! Thunder! The event of the year! I'll speak to 'em. Le' go a minute, Tom, will you?

MODERNA.

Stop, William dear, it's not that. I may go with you, but I wanted to go on the Rensselaers' drag.

WILLIAM, returning to the window.

What can it matter, as long as you see the match?

MODERNA.

You forget I'm not a schoolboy. I don't care for the match, but I do care who I go with. It's so dull to go with you, you can talk of nothing but the fielding, and you yelp so. I like to go on a drag, and have lunch, and see people. Oh, dear, why *did* mother need to invite a regular old *moiré antique* aunt, like her, to spoil everything, and interfere, and manage us all. It's all very well for you and father, you're men — I mean boys—and do as you like, but I have got to obey Aunt Eliza as if she was my mother, that's what mother said when she left.

WILLIAM, sententiously.

Girls want looking after.

MODERNA.

I'm far naughtier now that she is here, you don't *know* the things I've done, just because she forbids me. And she *will* call me Mary, and I am not used to it, and she orders everything for dinner I hate, and rice pudding for my looks, and she scolds the housemaids, and riles the cook, and she has turned the canaries out of the morning-room and sent my blue dress to be cleaned without asking me — William, you're not listening !

WILLIAM.

I'm so busy. .

MODERNA.

But, William, do listen ; you don't seem to see how I'm put upon.

WILLIAM.

I don't see what you have got to complain of. The Rensselaers are horrid. They came down to Eton last half to see Rensselaer—awful little smug, none of the fellows will know him—and I saw them

MODERNA.

But Aunt Eliza doesn't know about that. She only saw Flossie and her mother in the Park the other day, and thought "they didn't look respectable." Just because Flossie is pretty and well dressed !

WILLIAM.

Looks just like a chocolate box ! I say, you *are* interrupting me so ! (Raising his voice.) All right, old fellow ! (To Moderna.) There's Tom halloeing. I can't attend to you any more. (MODERNA twitches the string out of his mouth.) Let go—oh—ah—um—What a plague you are! *Do* go away!

MODERNA.

I hate you, William. (Goes slowly towards the door.) He *is* a selfish pig. I wish Peggy and Verona were home from school! They would think of something. (Stops in front of the pier-glass.) I like this dress, it's the prettiest I've had. It fits me. It's far too good to walk round and round the enclosure with William and Tom Riddell—that's what it would be. Oh, it's too mean! (Shakes her fist in the direction of her aunt's pin-cushion.) I hope, yes, I hope she will have toothache to-night. She wants punishing. (Takes a small bottle out of the dressing-case.) I'll hide the laudanum. No, wait—(she empties the contents out of the window, puts it back, and takes out another bottle) I've got it, I'll make her sit up. (She drinks. She daubs her face with Bloom of Ninon.) There! I think I look pretty ghastly! Oh, I wish Cecilia were here, she would enjoy it so!

Enter Aunt ELIZA.

AUNT ELIZA.

Oh, Mary! You here! You are dressed to go, I see. So that's your costume, is it? A little too showy, isn't it? In my days, girls—

MODERNA.

—Were dowdy. But it doesn't matter. (Gloomily.) I am going to take it off—if I have strength to. I couldn't go to the match *now*, even if I wanted. (Stares fixedly at the laudanum bottle.) You'll miss it to-night, when you have toothache.

AUNT ELIZA.

Miss what?

MODERNA.

Your laudanum.

AUNT ELIZA.

Mercy, child!

MODERNA.

You drove me to it. I've swallowed it. May you be forgiven. Break it to them gently. (Sinks on to the sofa.)

AUNT ELIZA, wildly.

Gervaise! William! Here! Mary says (WILLIAM turns round) that she has taken poison.

WILLIAM, coming away from the window languidly.

She's only "ragging"! Look here, Mod, how dare you frighten Aunt Eliza so? It's not nice of you. Drop it.

MODERNA, sulkily.

It's not nice of her. She's the unkindest aunt I ever heard of, and I hope we shall meet in heaven, but I don't believe we shall. Oh, my poor head! . . .

AUNT ELIZA.

Here's the bottle, William, it's empty. There was half left from last night, what am I to do, William? Your father's out. Send—send for Pooley. (Flies to the bell.)

WILLIAM, sagely examining the bottle.

Excuse me, aunt. Will you leave this matter to me?

AUNT ELIZA.

But you are only a lad—

WILLIAM.

Excuse me, Aunt—an Eton fellow! Kindly leave it all to me. I know chemistry. She's not had enough to hurt her. Freeman Mudford at m' tutor's did the very same thing last half, and we just lammed it into him with knotted towels all night, and kept him awake, I promise you. (MODERNA starts.) Keep her awake, that's all. Get some strong coffee made — um — um — (MODERNA listens anxiously.) Send for Pooley if you like, but I assure you that there is no need. I know how to manage these sort of cases.

MODERNA, sings, in a pathetic Ophelia-like manner·

" Sleep, little baby, do-oo-nt you cry !
You'll be an angel by and by." . . .

AUNT ELIZA, awestruck.

What is she singing, William ?

WILLIAM.

Some sentimental rot. Oh, dry up, Moderna !

MODERNA.

I always thought you went in for good manners at Eton. (Rises and comes forward.) Please, Aunt Eliza, give mother my love when she comes back. I have not been a very dutiful daughter to her—

WILLIAM.

I should think not.

MODERNA.

Shut up, you! Please Aunt, ask her to try to think
kindly of me when I am gone, and not weep for me·
I've made my will—it's in the left-hand pigeon-hole of
my desk.   I did leave all my jewellery to Calder-
Marston, but now I want Peggy and Verona to have it
equally—quite equally, or they will fight, I know them. . . .

WILLIAM, hums.

" Give my chewing gum to sister,
I shall never want it more."

AUNT ELIZA.

Be quiet, bad boy!   Are you sure you are doing right?
I can't have my brother's child die on my hands.   And
she does look dreadfully excited, poor thing . . . her eyes
are quite bright. . . .

WILLIAM, meaningly.

H'm ! Mudford's were all glazey and fishy. . . .

MODERNA, aside, uneasily.

I wish I had had time to look up the symptoms.   (Aloud.)
Aunt, my features won't be distorted, I fancy.   I shall
pass away quite quietly.   Put snowdrops on my grave
. . . ah . . . for I died young.   (Sinks back.)

AUNT ELIZA.

Oh, William, she's going off !   Save her !

WILLIAM.

Here, take a corner of this towel and tie a knot in it,
and flick—

D

MODERNA.

No, no, I won't be flicked, it would ruin my frock. Oh, do let me die quietly! Quietly, I say; don't joggle me so.

WILLIAM.

Here, Aunt, take one arm and I'll take the other. It will ruin your dress as you say, Moderna, but we can't let you die. (They hale her up and down.)

MODERNA.

You hurt me, William. Can't you leave me alone? Nothing you can do will save me. What will they all say —what will Cecilia say (chokes with laughter) when they hear?

AUNT ELIZA.

This is dreadful! These convulsive sobs— (Wringing her hands.) Oh, if I had only known what would happen, I should have let her go a thousand times over. I should not have interfered. Your mother never told me of Mary's headstrong character—she should have warned me of it before I took charge of her. William, she looks worse and worse! That deadly pallor. . . .
(MODERNA again chokes with laughter. Aunt ELIZA threatens hysterics.)

WILLIAM.

I say, how's a fellow to manage both of you? Aunt, do go away and fetch the cook; I'm tired, and my arms are nearly tugged off. There, do go, or you'll faint.

Exit Aunt ELIZA.

MODERNA, aloud.

William, leave go of my arm. (Aside.) Shall I tell him?
No, it's such fun. (Aloud.) Look here, I'm not going to
be dictated to by a mere boy. You don't understand, I
want to be left alone, to make my peace with heaven
and say my prayers, and think about good things.

WILLIAM.

Ah, but you might fall asleep thinking of them, as you
do in Chapel, when you come down. I've seen you.

MODERNA.   .

Oh dear, oh dear, I must have walked miles !

WILLIAM.

Can't say. Haven't got a pedometer. Will you have
the towels, then ?

MODERNA.

No, I won't, I'm going to sit down. I'm dead tired.

WILLIAM.

So am I, as tired as if I'd had a football scrimmage.
It's no joke keeping girls alive, I can tell you.

MODERNA, sitting down, and splitting with laughter.

Oh, William, you are the most absurd boy, and you do
think yourself so very clever, don't you ? Wouldn't the
fellows just laugh at you if they knew how you had
been taken in by a *girl* ?

WILLIAM.

What, didn't you take laudanum ?

MODERNA.

No, *Eau de Cologne.*

WILLIAM.

You wicked girl !

MODERNA.

You idiot !

WILLIAM.

You ought to be slapped.

MODERNA.

Don't you dare !

WILLIAM.

Do you think I'd condescend to touch a woman ?   But
somebody ought to.   And now I'll tell *you* something.
You didn't do it at all well—not like Freeman Mudford.
Any doctor would have seen in a moment that you were
ragging.   I didn't think it was the real thing, but of
course it is as well to be on the safe side . . . and spoilt
my morning with Tom !   What plagues girls are !

Re-enter Aunt ELIZA.

AUNT ELIZA.

William, what are you thinking of ?   You have let her
sit down !

WILLIAM.

I'm about sick of this.   Speak to her, ma'am.

MODERNA, brusquely.

So am I.   William, what o'clock is it?

WILLIAM.

Twelve o'clock.   Hallo! You seem pretty fit!

A SERVANT enters.

SERVANT.

Mrs. and Miss Rensselaer, called for Miss Maskelyne!

MODERNA.

There! I am going.   You said I might just now when
I was dying.   And I am ready dressed.   Hooray!
Explain, William, you are good at it.   I'm off.   Good-
bye, Aunt Eliza.   You can't say I'm disobeying you.
(Kisses the bewildered Aunt ELIZA effusively and goes off. WILLIAM explains.)

V

At MRS. RENSSELAER'S *bal masqué*. MODERNA and a PERFECT
STRANGER are sitting in the red-balze balcony. Down below is the
street, and rows of carriages and blinking, clinking hansoms.

THE PERFECT STRANGER.

Yes? . . . do go on. . . . It interests me intensely, and
there is really nothing odd in your telling a perfect
stranger all this.

MODERNA.

Is there not?   Well . . . so then he said—   There

he is, over there! As Masaniello! You are not looking!

THE PERFECT STRANGER.

I needn't look. I know the type. Please go on.

MODERNA.

Well then he said—you know, I have only met him three or four times—I don't believe he even knows my christian name!— "Then you really and truly meant nothing?" and I said, "Nothing, believe me! I am very sorry this has happened!" and he said quite bitterly, "Women always say that!" and I said, rather bitterly too, of course, "Oh, do they? Then you know from experience?" So he said, "That cheap cynicism is quite unworthy of you! but I will tell you the truth; you are literally the first woman I have ever spoken of love to."

THE PERFECT STRANGER.

And did he go down in your estimation?

MODERNA, blushing.

Yes—rather—but that's not the point! "You are the first woman, etc., and I don't think there will ever be another."

THE PERFECT STRANGER.

He *doesn't think!* Cautious young Oxford!

MODERNA.

So I said, "Oh, don't say that, Mr. Donkin, there are lots of nicer girls in the world."

THE PERFECT STRANGER.

I have heard that phrase before.

MODERNA.

Yes, I know; but somehow in those sort of situations
one uses the stock phrases—at least I do.

THE PERFECT STRANGER.

Unless— ?

MODERNA.

You interrupt! Then he got up, and he looked years
older (which was an advantage), and stared hard at me,
and he said, "Those eyes—they lied—they said— " I
was cross, and I said quickly, "Well, what did they say?
I am not going to be made responsible for them. They
didn't say I cared for you, I am sure! You are not
going to make out that I have done you any harm in
the short time I have known you?" Then he got very
angry, and he said, "You have done what you never
can undo. You have taken the love of a man, and all
the time you did not want it. My first love—I gave it
you freely, and I never can give it again! It has gone
for ever from me—my beautiful boy's love." Wasn't
that maddening? I said directly I hadn't asked him for
his beautiful boy's love, and that I was sure there was
some of it left, and that he was to take me back to my
mother, for I wanted to go home at once.

THE PERFECT STRANGER.

And you were really going to pay him that compliment?

MODERNA.

It seemed the proper thing to do. It would have been so heartless to go on dancing—

THE PERFECT STRANGER.

On a broken heart! Well, you know the ethics of these matters. But you didn't go! You compromised matters by sitting out with me, and telling me all about it?

MODERNA, piteously.

Oh, it is dreadful! I don't know you, and yet—you make me tell you things.

THE PERFECT STRANGER.

Women sometimes do. (Smiling.)

MODERNA.

Is it that you mesmerise them?

THE PERFECT STRANGER.

Don't talk such dreadful nonsense, please.

MODERNA.

Well the "empire of a strong mind over a weak one?"

THE PERFECT STRANGER.

Are you weak? You do not know if I am strong. I am a perfect stranger to you. But shall I tell you why you have spoken to me so frankly?

MODERNA.

Yes, tell me, for I haven't the slightest idea.

THE PERFECT STRANGER.

In the first place, because to-night you are not quite yourself—your society self, I mean. You are, without knowing it, a little infected by the romance of the *bal masqué* — you breathe for a time the atmosphere of a different artificial world, in which all things are possible—till the Cinderella hour of twelve o'clock ! You are excited by light and noise and music, you hardly know what you are saying, you are sincere in spite of yourself. If you were not a nice woman, you would be hateful, do you know ? In the second place, you *feel* you can trust me—you can have no means of *knowing*—and I have told you that in half an hour I bid you good-bye, and hail one of those jingling hansoms out there, and catch the 11.40 to Gravesend, for the *Vrynia*, which sails by morning tide. So I shall have no more communication with your world. I don't know your name and you don't know mine—I could tell it you if you liked !

MODERNA.

Don't.

THE PERFECT STRANGER.

I knew you would say that. You are wise. Now, can you not talk to me for half an hour as to one condemned to death ? You will be tolerably near the truth. Is it not good to talk to a man openly, for once, without prejudice ; to enjoy the friendship of an hour—a friend-

ship without past or future? I am a man, older than
you, not unversed in the ways of men—and of women !
(laughing.) I ought to be a sort of father-confessor to
you, with no power of absolution, it is true, but far
more secret than the grave—or a priest !

MODERNA.

I have a brother.

THE PERFECT STRANGER.

A brother ! A brother is half a father. A husband is
—useless too. Let me tell you, a man who is neither
brother, husband, nor lover, who can pass over a woman's
face in his haste to arrive at her soul, and speak to her
plainly; as it were two souls, spiritually and intellectu-
ally face to face—

MODERNA.

As you have to me. You don't speak to me as if I
were a woman. I like it . . . you don't even think me
pretty, do you?

THE PERFECT STRANGER.

No, but you will be ! Go on. Tell me how many
men—for they don't *all* forget you are a woman—how
many men have told you they loved you?

MODERNA, embarrassed.

I—

THE PERFECT STRANGER.

You think me impertinent, don't you?

MODERNA.

Yes, rather.

THE PERFECT STRANGER, coolly.

Very, in fact.   But then you are at perfect liberty not
to answer my questions?

MODERNA.

I know I need not—I know I ought not to—but I shall.

THE PERFECT STRANGER.

I know you will.

MODERNA.

And supposing I were to get up and walk across the
room to my mother, and leave you?

THE PERFECT STRANGER.

Yes, you ought.   I see your mother.   I know her by
her likeness to you.   She is over there eating an
ice, all unconscious of blame.   Shall I take you to
her?

MODERNA.

What would you think of me if I said "yes?"

THE PERFECT STRANGER.

That you were behaving as a well-brought-up young
lady should do, under the circumstances.   I should
bow, and regret that I was not a dancing-man, and
could not have the pleasure, etc.

MODERNA, suddenly.

Why do you come to balls?

THE PERFECT STRANGER.

I suppose in the vague hope of meeting some day with a real woman, and talking to her. It is one of the very few social opportunities one has of doing so. A dinner party is complicated with eating—how can two immortal souls communicate with each other through a medium of steaming soup, or the fumes of the roast, or at a *musicale* where one is constantly "hushed," until one's blood boils? But at a dance, social convention has decreed that one should have a woman to oneself for a quarter of an hour at least. I singled you out at once, and hoped that you would let me speak to you—I *was* introduced, wasn't I?

MODERNA, smiling.

As the Prince of Abyssinia.

THE PERFECT STRANGER.

To the Nut-brown Maid. But I should have spoken to you anyhow—such is my arrogance.

MODERNA.

Am *I* a real woman?

THE PERFECT STRANGER.

Ah, you hark back! That is like a woman. Yes, you are a real woman, but a very young one. I suppose I ought not to have spoken to you as I have done. You are a strange mixture.   You have the *naïveté* of a child, the wayward mouth of a child, but—your eyes—as that unhappy youth said in his jargon of the affections— your eyes are not the eyes of a child !   I wonder what will be the end of you ?   The conventional one, I suppose ?

MODERNA.

I hope not.

THE PERFECT STRANGER.

How delightfully young of you !   You are—but unless I remain impersonal I shall become impertinent.   You know it was really *your* fault that we ever left the serene heights of abstraction ; like a true woman, you always brought the subject home.   Well, ask me any questions you like.   I can give you any amount of bad advice.

MODERNA, laughing.

Do,

THE PERFECT STRANGER.

Ah, you don't want any advice.   Your path is not devious as yet.   But . . . the world goes on, though I shall be out of it.   (Suddenly.)   Your rule of life is simple. Find a man you can love and trust, and then—

MODERNA.

What ?

THE PERFECT STRANGER.

Don't marry him !

MODERNA.

Do you mean I should make him miserable ?   Oh, you are horribly cynical !

THE PERFECT STRANGER, smiling.

I scorn to be.   It is the refuge of the mental destitute.
But I think I am getting tired.   Did I tell you I was
an invalid?

MODERNA.

I guessed.

THE PERFECT STRANGER.

And that is why you were so indulgent, and patient with
my wild talk?   Tell me, are you sorry you met me?
Please answer quickly.

MODERNA.

Why?

THE PERFECT STRANGER.

Because I am going to say good-bye.   It is eleven
o'clock.   I must think of my train. . . .   Where shall I
take you?

MODERNA.

Oh, don't take me anywhere.

THE PERFECT STRANGER.

I wish I could take. . . .   No, I don't. . . .   Not take
you back to your mother, you say?

MODERNA.

I had rather not.   Leave me here.

THE PERFECT STRANGER.

And go straight from you without saying good-bye to
any one else?   I understand.   Then I shall have no

opportunity of asking your name. What cowards women are !

MODERNA, sharply.

You don't know anything about women. My name is Mary Elizabeth Maskelyne.

THE PERFECT STRANGER.

It represents nothing to me. But I apologise for what I said. Do you forgive me ?

MODERNA.

Of course. And are you really going ?

THE PERFECT STRANGER.

I should spoil it if I stayed. . . . Good-bye !

LATER.

MODERNA, to Miss RENSSELAER.

Who was the man dressed as the Prince of Abyssinia ?

MISS RENSSELAER.

Sir Richard Vyse, the famous metaphysician. He is quite mad, they say, and dying of consumption. Half a lung and that sort of thing. Can't live six months. I'll introduce you to his doctor, who is here as Rasselas.

MODERNA.

No, don't.

·   MISS RENSSELAER.

Didn't you like Sir Richard ?

MODERNA.

He's rather bad form. . . .   (Miss RENSSELAER passes on.)
Now, how could I say that ? when I am—yes, I *am* sorry
I shall never see him again !   But it *was* impertinent of
him to catechise me in that way, and very idiotic of me
to answer.   But it was very interesting.   That's the
worst of it.   Life would be so much more amusing if
one wasn't obliged to keep up one's dignity.   The
moment a man says anything he shouldn't, one has to
snub him.   But one would like to hear it, all the same.

.

VI

IN the Atelier of Monsieur FESTUGÈRES at Chelsea.   Young men in
blouses ; young girls in pinafores ; easels, canvases, an all-pervading
smell of turpentine.

A GIRL'S VOICE.

Oh, I say, bother this square touch !   I can't get into
it at all.   I'd rather do pastel any day.

A MAN'S VOICE.

Flashy clap-trap !   Do take some pains with this, you've
got it in you to do it, you know.

A GIRL'S VOICE.

No, I shall never get it.   (Sighs.)

A MAN'S VOICE.

Let's see ! . . . That's very clever, what you have done ! Carry it a little further.

A GIRL'S VOICE.

That's just it — I can't.   Oh, do, do, do a little bit of that shoulder blade for me, just to show me !

A MAN'S VOICE.

Charmed !   (A silence.)

A GIRL'S VOICE.

How do you like Mr. Carter's composition ?   Isn't it like Miss Vane ?

A MAN'S VOICE.

On Tuesday he came here early, you know . . . and I caught him with his nose buried in her turpentiny apron as it hung on the nail. . . . Oh, I beg your pardon, what have I done ?

A GIRL'S VOICE, laughing.

Knocked over *my* turpentine with your great " square touch."

A MAN'S VOICE.

You needn't chaff a fellow because he is only eighteen and has big hands.

A GIRL'S VOICE.

Yes, and can paint with them, which is more than I can do with my little ones.

E

A MAN'S VOICE.

See now . . . you put it on just so . . .

A GIRL'S VOICE.

But I want to hear some more about Miss—

FESTUGÈRES, suddenly from the other end of the room, where he is occupied in perpetrating extraordinary manœuvres with a pen-knife and a red silk handkerchief, on a girl's drawing.

Pscht ! Pscht ! Silence ! (A silence as of the grave sets in. FESTUGÈRES continues in meditative accents.) Il me semble toujours entendre les tons argentins de Mademoiselle Maskelyne! Je vous prie bien, Mademoiselle, de garder votre argot sociale pour le salon de Madame votre mère. . . . Qu'est ce que vous fabriquez la bas ?

. MODERNA.

Oh, Monsieur Festugères, do come to me, I'm in such a muddle !

FESTUGÈRES.

Allons, voyons ! . . . Mais vous savez, ce n'est pas mal du tout. C'est d'une admirable fidélité. (Mutters.) Le talent y est — c'est bien l'enthousiasme qui manque. (Shrugs his shoulders and passes on.)

A MAN'S VOICE.

Miss Maskelyne—

MODERNA.

Oh, don't speak to me, or he will be down on us again ! I am going to work like a nigger for the next couple of hours. (She works for an hour. At the end of that time her head drops on to the rim of her easel. . . . Miss PARKER leans across from hers.)

*   *   *   *   *

MISS PARKER, severely.

Miss Maskelyne, you have been asleep!

MODERNA, rubbing her eyes.

Oh, don't scold me, Parker dear, I was dancing till four this morning.

MISS PARKER, setting her palette carefully.

Yes, it was a very picturesque pose, and I felt an insane desire to sketch you . . . but honestly now, do you think that your being up till four in the morning is any excuse for coming here in such a state?

MODERNA.

My dear, one would think I was tipsy, to hear you.

MISS PARKER.

Well, I do consider it a form of intemperance. You go out every night, and come here for a few hours every day and doze between two balls—it is not an edifying spectacle. What an outsider you are! You seem to have no idea that life means work, life—

MODERNA.

" Life is real, life is earnest!"—how I hate that poem!

MISS PARKER, drily.

It doesn't appeal to social butterflies like you. Oh, it's too bad! These men and these women are here to make their lives, to earn their living; it is deadly earnest

to them. . . . Then you come in, in lovely frocks, with
an atmosphere of the ball-room clinging about you, and
distract us and demoralise us all by your prettiness—for
you are awfully pretty, my artistic eyes see that; pretty
enough to suborn a hanging committee or pervert a
president. . . . It's unfair, I say. It is amateurs like
you that choke up the avenues to fame and encumber
the ways of art.

MODERNA.

Parker, you talk like a book !

MISS PARKER, abruptly.

What do you come here for, I wonder ?

MODERNA, mildly.

I come to paint, I suppose.

MISS PARKER.

Paint ! You paint ! You have an unholy facility, I
must admit ; it is quite maddening sometimes to us poor
plodders to see you get your effect with the minimum of
trouble where some of us mug away for days and don't
even get it then. But mark me, it is only the first stage ;
you will stop there—there the trouble begins ; with the
real hard work; and *that* you are incapable of. You'll
never do anything ! Look at Miss Lane over there,
with her mock pearls and bare neck, and fourpenny-
three-farthings-a-yard muslin pinafore, and hair like a
bird's nest ! That girl has more art in her little finger
than you in your whole body !

MODERNA.

Go on, dear.

MISS PARKER.

Oh, I know I'm rude. I'm only a Bohemian, and Irish
at that. But, I tell you, I respect Miss Lane. What
do you think she does when she goes home? Do you
fancy she goes to balls and parties like you? No, she
spoils her eyes over a bedroom candle doing black and
white, and drawing herself in the looking-glass over and
over again for practice. She never has time to flirt.

MODERNA.

I suppose that means that I do.

MISS PARKER.

Oh yes, we are not so utterly beneath contempt, but
that you condescend—in a kind of Lady Clara Vere de
Vere way, to make us fall in love with you. You break
an artist's heart, for pastime, ere you go home to lunch.
You can't help it. You fascinate us all. You fascinate
me. It gives me quite a position in the studio that you
should choose me for your "pal." Irene Hand is so
jealous of me she won't speak to me hardly. She adores
you ; and look at the harm you've done her—Philips was
her devoted slave for years, and they used to travel here
from Putney together. Now he comes alone on the
bare chance of meeting you on the doorstep. Look at
young Valentine ! He has got his way to make by art,
and he thinks more of the privilege of washing your
brushes for you than— Oh, it is too bad of you !

MODERNA, sulkily.

I'm going to wash them myself. It's three now.

MISS PARKER, scornfully.

Going to chuck up already? (Relenting.) Here, let me do them for you !

MODERNA.

No. (They go into an inner room.)

MISS PARKER, meditatively.

What a pretty ring that is ! I should think turpentine isn't good for turquoises. They are not a present from Valentine, are they ? he couldn't afford turquoises. . . .

MODERNA, suddenly.

What do you want me to do ?

MISS PARKER.

Work, dear Lady Clara, and let the honest yeoman go, or else—

MODERNA.

What ?

MISS PARKER, bluntly.

Go yourself.

MODERNA.

I was thinking of it. But it is rather hard on me. You know I can't help—

MISS PARKER.

Yes, I know you can't help people falling in love with you. Do you try ? (Curiously.) Why does Frank Graham look so glum always, and why do you never speak to him now?

MODERNA.

Because . . . he once proposed. . . .

MISS PARKER.

How many have, if it isn't impertinent to ask?

MODERNA.

I really don't know . . . I mean . . . I can't help it *here* . . . in society I can.   They waylay me, as I go out, and they are all so silly and unpractical.

MISS PARKER, oracularly.

If Dick Valentine doesn't get his composition, he's done.

MODERNA, impulsively.

I'll go down to Stickleby, to my cousin Cecilia's, at once!

MISS PARKER, incredulously.

And miss the rest of your term here?

MODERNA.

Oh, I don't care . . . after what you have said . . . I shan't be an artist now.

MISS PARKER.

Well, dear Miss Maskelyne, to tell you the truth—

MODERNA.

Do, do.

MISS PARKER.

I think you draw very nicely . . . but I don't think you would ever be an artist.

MODERNA, despairingly.

I must be something.

MISS PARKER.

You'll be *somebody*, and that's better. You'll marry and have a house, and a position, and affect your generation that way. Leave Art to us poor things who can never have a lover. It .is everything to us. It is only a fashionable amusement to you. Oh, and don't be cross ; I never had any manners, and I have been saying outrageous things to you. Forgive me ! but I feel so strongly about you lovely amateurs ! Here comes Festugères back from his lunch. I must go and get his final verdict on my *pastel.* Wait for me. I'll walk part of the way home with you if I may. (Slips back again to her easel. MODERNA idly plays with her tools. Young VALENTINE timidly approaches her.)

YOUNG VALENTINE.

Miss Maskelyne, may I have a few words with you ?

MODERNA.

I'm afraid not, Mr. Valentine. I am going home almost immediately with Miss Parker.

YOUNG VALENTINE.

Cannot I speak to you on a matter of urgent importance one moment in the cloak room ?

MODERNA.

No, you can't—really. (Severely.) *Do* go and mind
your work. It's so much more important to you than
anything else. (Aside.) Parker is right. It's time I left.

NEXT DAY.

THE LUNCHEON HOUR.   IN THE GIRLS'
DRESSING-ROOM.

THE GIRL IN A PINK PINAFORE.

Hi, Brown! A packet of grey stumps, and three penny-
worth of milk, and two sheets of French paper, and a
Bath bun—how much is that?

THE PORTER.

Ten pence, Miss. I wish you'd keep them orders
distinct. It do muddle me so.

THE GIRL IN A PINK PINAFORE.

Don't be an ass, Brown. Here's a shilling. (Follows him
to the door.)

THE GIRL IN A BLUE PINAFORE.

I say, do you know, Miss Maskelyne is not coming
back any more?

THE GIRL IN A RED PINAFORE.

I say, who told you?

THE GIRL IN A BLUE PINAFORE.

Brown. She took all her traps away yesterday in a cab.

THE GIRL IN A RED PINAFORE.

Now we shall have some peace.

THE GIRL IN A PINK PINAFORE.

One got perfectly sick of the sound of her voice.

THE GIRL IN A RED PINAFORE.

She was always borrowing my H.B., and forgetting to return it.

THE GIRL IN A BLUE PINAFORE.

Who's going to return a stump like that?

THE GIRL IN A RED PINAFORE.

Five stumps make a pencil, I consider.

THE GIRL IN A BLUE PINAFORE.

She hadn't a spark of real talent.   Festugères used to work up her things for her, and make them presentable.

THE GIRL IN A PINK PINAFORE.

Oh—I say—that's not true, she would never let him.

THE GIRL IN A BLUE PINAFORE.

Too beastly conceited for that.

THE GIRL IN A PINK PINAFORE.

I shan't be able to finish my sketch of her.

THE GIRL IN A RED PINAFORE.

Oh, did you think her pretty?   Not at all picturesque.

THE GIRL IN A PINK PINAFORE.

Because she was tidy, eh?

THE GIRL IN A BLUE PINAFORE.

Too fashionable!

THE GIRL IN A RED PINAFORE.

Going to be married, I daresay.   Art soon goes to the wall then.

  *   *   *   *   *

IN THE MEN'S DRESSING-ROOM.

MR. BRIGGS, the cad of the school.

I say, you fellows, do you know little Maskelyne has left for good?

MR. MURGATROYD, the genius.

Not really?   What a bore!   We shall all go to sleep.

MR. SHEPHERD, the flirt.

Yes, it's no fun now.   Such an ugly set of girls left.

MR. GRAHAM, captain of the school.

I shall go to Paris.

MR. MURGATROYD.

She didn't draw badly—might have done something.

MR. GRAHAM.

Yes, if you fellows would have let her.

MR. BRIGGS.

An awful chatterbox!

MR. MURGATROYD.

But not a bit spiteful!

MR. GRAHAM.

A good hand at a caricature!

MR. SHEPHERD.

She's going to be married, of course.   I say . . .
Muggles . . . ?

MR. MURGATROYD.

Shut up, you ass.

MR. GRAHAM.

Here, I say, time's up!   Pose the model, some one!
Here come all the girls—and Festugères!   Look out
Briggs, you have put your "donkey" on my foot!

MR. BRIGGS.

Beg pardon! (To FESTUGÈRES, respectfully.) Has Miss Maskelyne left for good, sir?   Her locker is empty, and her
maid came for her pinafore this morning.

FESTUGÈRES.

Ah, ça vous intrigue tous? 'Rest tranquil.   Cette char-
mante Miss Maskelyne is gone—gone—how you say?
never come back no more—and now I shall hope for
some solid results.   Plus de distractions, eh?

MR. BRIGGS.

She wasn't much at working, was she, sir? Gracious
me! It used to amuse me to see little Maskelyne come
in and nod at the model, and sit down gracefully, and
sigh, and yawn, and do three strokes in three quarters
of an hour. These swell society girls are never any
good!

FESTUGÈRES, frowning.

Très bien, Monsieur, il suffit de la dénigrer, maintenant!
Pas de talent, vous dites? Eh bien, je vous conseille,
moi, d'en avoir autant. You may laugh, vous autres,
but I will tell you la vraie vérité. Elle manquait d'enthousiasme, d'application, c'est, ma foi, vrai, elle n'en-
tendait rien de la "sainte ardeur du travail" — belle
phrase de Rénan—mais elle avait—elle avait ça (snaps his
finger suggestively) et je vous en souhaite tous autant!
(Passes on with a contemptuous look at Mr. BRIGGS.)

MR. BRIGGS.

What's "ça"? (Imitating the gesture.)

TWO VOICES.

What you haven't got, my dear fellow.

MR. BRIGGS.

She has known how to get the soft side of old Festy,
at any rate.

MR. SHEPHERD.

I should say "that" meant a good French accent—

MR. GRAHAM.

And a good figure !

MR. BRIGGS.

Lots of damned cheek !

MR. SHEPHERD.

Plenty of " devil," in fact.

MR. MURGATROYD.

And that's another word for genius. (Wkh conviction.) Oh, I'm sure Festy didn't mean that !

VII

At Stickleby Hall, Yorkshire. It is about six o'clock. Cecilia Riddell is seated at her desk in her room. Enter Moderna, a little dusty, a little out of breath.

CECILIA, rising hastily.

My beloved cousin !   I am so glad . . . but we did not expect you till next week !

MODERNA.

No—I did not expect myself—but you said I might come when I liked—so I did—and Minching is down-stairs—and can you put us up?—and where is Aunt Riddell?

CECILIA.

I am not sure.   In the dairy perhaps—

MODERNA, laughing.

Or the fernery, or the piggery, or the hen-coop. I
should never expect to find her in the drawing-room.

CECILIA.

She hates sitting there, except when we have a meeting.

MODERNA, sitting down.

I should be awfully frightened of her, I think, if she
hadn't inherited some of her daughter's good qualities.

CECILIA, mildly.

How *can* she inherit from me, dear? Well, she will be
in presently, and delighted to see you. Where is your
luggage?

MODERNA.

Kicking its heels at the station. Please send. I walked
up. I came in the guard's van from Lee Junction.

CECILIA.

· How did you manage that?

MODERNA.

Got out at Lee—contrived to nearly miss the train—
jumped in as we moved off. And so the guard had to
keep me! He was so cross—but I soon soothed him!

CECILIA.

You funny girl! Well, I am glad to see you, though I
am in the middle of my holiday thesis, and—I must
break it to you—we are going out to-night. There is a

branch temperance meeting at Lee at seven, and I'm
secretary, and have to keep the minutes.

MODERNA.

Then I'll sit over the fire and read inferior novels. I've
been out every night for a week.

CECILIA.

Oh, no, you won't.   Captain Jekyll is here.

MODERNA.

I'm much too tired to cope with country squires.   Take
him with you.

CECILIA.

He wouldn't go.   He hates mother's temperance routs,
and our radicalism and all that—wonders everybody
doesn't leave this house a Tory and a drunkard! Rude,
isn't he?

MODERNA.

Then can't I go with you? (Aside.)   Oh, dear, what am
I proposing?

CECILIA.

Compose yourself, my friend—not room in the cart!
You'll just have to make up your mind to dine here
quietly with Frank.

MODERNA, with affected horror.

Tête-à-tête ?

CECILIA.

Now, Moderna, if you want to "rile" mother, let her
hear you allude to the effete institution of chaperons!

She goes out with me, but she has never *chaperoned* me in her life !

MODERNA.

Dear little thing ! With a Girton waist and sensible hair like that, it would be a bold man who would venture to flirt with you. Think—only twenty, and measure twenty-six round the waist ! And yet you manage to be pretty !

CECILIA.

I like to be comfortable; I don't care to figure in the society papers like you. Have you that black-and-white gown they described a month ago ?

MODERNA.

Yes, I hate it—tired of it.

CECILIA.

Put it on to-night. I should like to hear what Frank says about it.

MODERNA.

No, I shall not. I shall borrow one of your dresses and wind a Liberty sash five times round my waist. I shall do at Stickleby what Stickleby does. (Sitting down.) Now, look here, don't you want to hear all about Calder-Marston ? He's just going to bring out Titus Andronicus.

CECILIA.

I don't know that I am so much interested in Calder-Marston now. Girton knocked all that out of me. It was just a phase. They'd all had it.

F

MODERNA.

And Society knocked it out of me.   It was rather fun
though, while it lasted.

CECILIA.

It gave us a good many sleepless nights.

MODERNA.

Bad for the complexion, but good for the soul !   However, I saw him gluttonously eating his own and partner's
oysters at the Savoy one night, and that finished me !   I
went home and burnt all the photos I could find.

CECILIA.

And every second girl at Girton was in love with him.
It was *too* common.   I had an auction of all mine.

MODERNA.

Tout lasse, tout passe, tout casse.

Enter Lady RIDDELL with a large basket of eggs on her arm.   MODERNA
hastily slips off her rings before incurring her truculent hand-shake.

LADY RIDDELL.

Glad to see you, my dear.   Cecilia has doubtless in-
formed you of to-night's programme.   Very inhospitable !
Can't be helped !   Affairs of the country !   Can't take
you with us—not room.   'Pity !   'Done you good.

MODERNA.

I'm rather tired, aunt.

LADY RIDDELL.

Tired ! not you—at your age !   I never allow Cecilia to
say she is tired.   If she does, she knows what to expect.

CECILIA, in a low voice.

Bryonia. . . .

LADY RIDDELL.

You'll have to make up your mind to dine quietly with
Captain Jekyll.   Good heart—limited intellect !   A
very poor Radical—almost a Conservative.   Make the
best of him.   Don't flirt with him—or Cecilia will have
something to say to that.   'Must go and speak to the
bailiff.

Exit.

CECILIA, with concentrated venom.

I could kill mother !

MODERNA, laughing.

Don't, dear.   Such a loss to the cause !

CECILIA.

Why need she give me away like that ?

MODERNA.

But you don't mind me, do you, Cissy ?   You always
confided in me about Calder-Marston, you know.

CECILIA, slowly.

But this is different.

MODERNA.

Are you engaged ?

CECILIA.

No . . . but . . .

MODERNA.

You needn't say any more, darling.   " No " and " but "
are quite enough.   What are his advantages?   Is he
good-looking ?

CECILIA.

No—rather—yes—very.   *I* think so.

MODERNA.

Clever ?

CECILIA.

Yes—rather—well, no—not in your line at any rate.
He is the best shot and the straightest rider in the
county.

MODERNA.

Well off?

CECILIA.

Oh yes.   His property marches with ours—a ring
fence—

MODERNA.

Oh, the ring fence settles it.   You'll marry him, of
course.

CECILIA.

But he hasn't asked me.   (Shrieking.)   Moderna, he has
not asked me !   Remember that.   He most likely never
will.   Do take care—don't know anything—you are so
careless !

MODERNA.

Shall I flirt with him to prove that I am absolutely unaware of the state of affairs between you?

CECILIA, sadly.

And cut me out?

MODERNA.

You need not be afraid of that, dear. · He is sure not to be at all my sort.

CECILIA.

He's everybody's sort.

MODERNA.

That's rather a profound remark, though you don't know it. Handsome, ready, sharp, active— I know exactly the sort of man. All the same I shall not know what in the world to say to him—unless we can talk about you.

CECILIA.

Oh, Moderna, don't.

Enter Lady RIDDELL.

LADY RIDDELL.

Cecilia, the cart will be round exactly in five minutes. We shall have some sandwiches in the Committee room. Be quick.

CECILIA.

But, mother—

LADY RIDDELL.

But what?

CECILIA.

I should like to introduce Moderna to Frank before we
go and leave her . . .

LADY RIDDELL.

Fiddle-de-dee! The sooner that idiotic convention is
dropped the better. Walk up to the man and say, "I'm
Moderna Maskelyne. Who are you?" Eat a good
dinner, and enjoy yourself. Go to bed early. (The gong
is sounded.) See you in the morning—breakfast at eight-
thirty. There you are! Good-night.

Exit.

CECILIA, whispers.

Only Kop's Ale, dear, or lemonade! Make out with
brandy-cherries! That's what Flossie Rensselaer does
when she stays here.

Exit.

*   *   *   *   *

MODERNA, on her way downstairs.

Too bad! Three hours' *tête-à-tête*. Just like Aunt
Riddell! And what on earth am I to say to a horsey
and doggy man? I don't know a thing about one or
the other. (Hums.)

>   " But native cheek, where facts were weak,
>   Pulled him in triumph through."

IX

IN the long gallery at Stickleby Hall. It is half-past ten o'clock.

MODERNA, sitting in the window-seat.

I wish I were dead !

* * * * *

A man has kissed me !

* * * * *

There it is ! (Rubbing her cheek.) Nothing can ever take it away now. I can't think how it happened . . . I can't, I can't. I never thought such a thing would happen to me !

* * * * *

Is there anything dreadful about me ? Do I look the kind of girl men kiss for fun ? Like a bar-maid or an actress ? No, I don't. I look serious. I look as if no man had ever kissed me ; and no man ever did till now.

* * * * *

He has insulted me. I ought to hate him. And the worst of it is, I don't. No, I don't. If I had hated him, I shouldn't have let him do it, for it wasn't exactly against my will . . . and yet I didn't for a moment expect him to . . . insult me. He has !

* * * * *

And after all what is a kiss, to be so miserable about ? A mere peck—on my cheek, such as my brother William gives me, or my cousin Cecilia ! Why should I mind ?

* * * * *

But it was a man—a strange man! And now if ever I fall in love—if any one ever falls in love with me—I shall have to tell him that I have been kissed! I can never give him the first . . . I've given it to a mere stranger, and I can never give it again. So I shall never marry—that settles it. I didn't mean to, but I couldn't now, if I wanted to.

*   *   *   *   *

How did it happen? I am confused. I don't seem to remember. Did I flirt with him? I sang to him—that's not flirting. But I never sang so . . . so. . . . Then he came out with me and gave me my candle . . . and then he looked at me, I remember his eyes. They were so dark. I looked at them. I wish I hadn't. . . . Then we shook hands . . . and then. . . . (She hides her face.) I ran away. I didn't give him time to say anything. I wonder how he looked! Did he think I was angry, or did he think—? Perhaps he smiled! *Now* I hate him. (Clenches her hands.) He has kissed me! (Sobs.)

Captain JEKYLL comes slowly upstairs and suppresses an exclamation on seeing the figure on the window-seat. She raises her head and darts in the direction of her room. Her dress catches.

CAPTAIN JEKYLL, stiffly.

Let me—! (Disengages her dress. She submits.) There, you are free! Good-night. (He looks at her.) Good heavens, you are crying! What a brute I have been!

MODERNA.

Don't speak of it. Good-night!

CAPTAIN JEKYLL.

But I must.

MODERNA.

Don't you see that your speaking only makes it worse?
Oh go, go away—it is the best thing you can do.

CAPTAIN JEKYLL.

I know.   I would do anything to convince you! . . .
Look here, I shall be off to-morrow before breakfast, so
could you shake hands with me, and say you forgive me?

MODERNA, eagerly.

And will you really go?   How good of you!

CAPTAIN JEKYLL.

But you must shake hands with me first.

MODERNA.

I had so much rather not.

CAPTAIN JEKYLL.

Then you don't forgive me?

MODERNA.

I do, I do, only—I don't want to see your face.   I
don't want to be reminded of—my disgrace.

CAPTAIN JEKYLL.

Miss Maskelyne, there is no disgrace to you!   *I* shall
never forgive myself—but you—you must not for one
moment imagine that I construed your kindness to me

to-night into any form of encouragement. I was mad—
perfectly mad for five minutes. Won't you forgive me?
Say you'will?

MODERNA, wearily.

Yes, oh yes. . . .

CAPTAIN JEKYLL.

And will you forget?

MODERNA, violently.

I can't, I can't. I shall think of it, and be ashamed for
all the rest of my life. Good-night. (Going.)

CAPTAIN JEKYLL, slowly.

Then there is only one thing to be done now, that I
can see. . . .

MODERNA.

There is nothing to be done. Oh, do let it rest.
Good-night.

CAPTAIN JEKYLL, still hesitatingly.

Listen to me one moment, Miss Maskelyne. What I
propose is . . . that you should . . . become engaged to
me! Would it be so very impossible?

A Pause.

MODERNA, coldly.

It is very good of you to think of it—but I don't see
that there is any advantage to be gained by our both
making ourselves miserable for life.

CAPTAIN JEKYLL, hotly.

I can answer for it that it would not make *me* miserable.
Try it! Listen—I must not say I love you, you whom
I've only known five hours—but upon my soul—that
word more nearly expresses what I feel than any other
I could use. I wish I could make you believe me . . .
dear?

MODERNA, aside.

I almost wish you could. (Aloud.) Thank you. (Laughing
bitterly.) I suppose it is all right now. You have proposed to me, and I have refused you. What more could
I want? I ought to be satisfied. I am. I will shake
hands and say good-night.

CAPTAIN JEKYLL.

For heaven's sake, take me seriously! I never was
more serious in my life—or more in love. It is true,
on my honour. No woman in the world ever was to me
what you are. (Takes her hand, she does not draw it away.) Don't
you see, dear, it settles it all? There is no harm in
being kissed by the man you are going to marry. We
won't say anything about it yet. It would seem rather
sudden, and startle them . . . but in a few days. . . . Lady
Riddell will be pleased . . . and Cecilia. . . .

MODERNA, suddenly.

Cecilia! Oh, what am I doing? Cecilia—and you—

CAPTAIN JEKYLL.

Why should you couple our names together. I am
nothing, and can never be anything to Cecilia.

MODERNA.

Nothing to Cecilia! But you are—you must be! I
mean . . . let me go . . .

CAPTAIN JEKYLL, holding her.

Not without yes or no! (The noise of wheels is heard.) Here
they are! (Hastily.) Give me an answer to-morrow. I
won't have one to-night. I must go and help them in.
Good-night, my darling. I would give the world to
repeat my offence—but not unless you give me leave.
I— Don't speak—good-night!

*   *   *   *   *

The morning after. Breakfast. Lady RIDDELL and CECILIA seated. Enter
Captain JEKYLL.

LADY RIDDELL.

Tea or coffee, Francis?

CAPTAIN JEKYLL.

Coffee, please. Where is Miss Maskelyne?

LADY RIDDELL.

Oh, don't ask me—gone off to London by the 8.20.

CAPTAIN JEKYLL.

Without leaving a message?

LADY RIDDELL.

Came to my bedside at seven, and wished me good-bye.
'Looked like a ghost. 'Said she must go up to town at
once. 'Gave some silly reason or other. Most extraordinary girl!

CECILIA, pettishly.

I call it very unkind of her.

LADY RIDDELL.

Oh, my niece is mad—plenty of charm—but quite mad !
That is what I always say.

CAPTAIN JEKYLL, savagely.

I quite agree with you, Lady Riddell.

X

IN the Vicarage Garden at Merrow, Surrey.   A tea-table spread under
the trees.   A game of tennis going on in the distance.

PEGGY.

Well I'm glad I'm not in that game.   I'm too good to
play with muffs.   Moderna has to take all Arthur
Deverel's balls first for fear he misses them, and Verona
is so busy talking to Tom Lawrence that she forgets to
play up.   I don't know why they call it tennis; I call it
talk.   Grown-up people like talk better than anything in
the world, it seems to me.   Mother and Mrs. Jenkyn
have gone in.   Mrs. Jenkyn is mad because she can't
play tennis.   She can do everything but that.   Her
waist 's too tight, and her heels too high.   Verona's glad
she's gone in, I can see.   Verona hates her.   Oh, these
grown-up people !

People are always asking me don't I wish I was out ?

Not if I know it! What should I want to be out
for?

They' don't understand. They say, "Poor thing,
only fifteen! Three long years to wait, and don't I wish
it was me when I see the girls ready dressed for a ball?"
No, thank you. I'm happier as I am. I know what
coming out is. I've seen two.

It's a horrid business, any way. First they order a
dress, and you'd think it was going to be the only dress
in the world, instead of a very simple affair—trimmed
daisies. Then when it comes home there's a scene.
They cry. It isn't right. It's hideous. They'd rather
die than wear it. There is no time to alter it—the
dressmaker takes care of that. Then they *must* do their
hair a different way, because they're "out." It isn't
used to it, and it won't stay up. They fuss—they
bounce about—they keep the carriage waiting—they
douse on oceans of powder, and forget to dust it off.
Then they come home, and lie on my bed in their ball
dresses, and kick about, and make it uncomfortable for
me, and say that society is a hollow fraud, and nothing
ever happens as you think it will. I could have told
them that. They only mean that they at once fixed
their affections on the most impossible man in the room,
and that he was never introduced to them—or that he
only danced once with them instead of twenty-one
times. *I* don't think life is a hollow fraud. I always
get what I want, but grown-up girls seem to expect such
a lot.

I wonder if I could eat another *petit four?* I've had
six, but then William has had eight. We were begin-

ning to make the dish look silly, so I sent him away to
field for balls. He was cross. He's a year older than
me. He's at Eton. Poor Eton! I manage him of
course. I manage everybody. It's all my doing that
we took this sweet vicarage for three months, and didn't
go to Folkestone or Eastbourne, or some other unearthly
place. There is never anything for me to do there, and
I bore myself to extinguishers. But here there are
woods and tool sheds and runaway bulls and everything
exciting, and not too many old frumps to come and call.

There are only the Deverels, and they're at Dunse
Court, a mile off. Fine old county family—don't they
just know it? The old lady's terrible, but I don't
trouble about her much, except to stick teasel balls in
her train when she isn't looking. Almeria, the girl, never
says anything; and as for the boys, Arthur and Fred—
well, Billy Danvers is worth a hundred of them.

I don't know which I think the handsomest! Fred,
I think. I'd rather have *him* for a brother-in-law—only
he's engaged to Flossie Rensselaer. That must have
been a bitter pill to old Lady Deverel. Flossie's a bit larky.
I mean to see a good deal of her when she is married.

What an awfully long game! Why don't they play
'vantage all? I daren't suggest it, for it might interfere
with their arrangements. I'll just have some more tea,
I think.

Oh, blow! The kettle isn't properly spliced! I
forgot to put the pin back. There's a mess! I'll lay
my handkerchief over the place. I wish it was cleaner!
What did I use it for? Oh, I remember, I carried
those tadpoles in it.

There, Moderna's put her foot through her best lace
petticoat! I knew she would. I told her she was an
idiot to wear it—nobody would see it. Of course when
you have a tumble, a lace petticoat comes very handy ;
but why tumble? Her frock's much too good, too, but
I suppose she had her reasons.

It doesn't in the least matter what I wear, only I
have to be very particular about my shoes, for, naturally,
they are the only things that show. I always wear these
plain white muslin frocks. They go to the wash regu-
larly once a week, with the window blinds. Yes, I know
my dress is short—very short! People think the girls
do it to keep me down. Nothing of the kind! It's my
own plan. If it was long I should have to behave, and
I don't want to, yet. It's such fun, now, when I make
an awful speech—as awful as I can—people stare, and
put up their eye-glasses and think, What a dreadful girl !
Then they look right down till they come to my feet,
and they see I'm only a school-girl, and don't know any
better, and are quite amused. I do know better—I
know a great deal better than I practise.

Of course I have beastly lessons to do, and all that.
I manage very nicely. " I do them, I do them, and it
doesn't take me long." I think the woman who has
come to my time of life without knowing how to get
round her lessons is a fool. People call me a little devil
sometimes, but they never call me a fool. I should
like to see them ! I don't object to " devil " at all.

I've got a governess. She's French. She is quite
harmless. I chose her carefully. I rather like her.
She knows I don't like her to interfere with me. I see

very little of her. I have my meals in the schoolroom with her. She reads novels all the time. I know they're improper—the girls say so—but I really have not time to investigate. Perhaps I should not understand them. I'm always in a hurry. I gobble. She says I'll spoil my complexion. I say, all right, I'll look after my complexion when the time comes.

We give dinner parties in town. When we happen to be thirteen I dine down. Mother says people are so superstitious. *She* is. We often happen to be thirteen, I like dining down for a change, though, as a matter of fact, I get more to eat on the stairs. The servants jolly well know they've not got to miss out a single dish, except the mutton. I can do without that. The other day I persuaded Billy Danvers to have hay fever, when he was engaged to dine here. He was fourteenth, for I got hold of the list. He did it, dear boy, to oblige me. But he came in in the evening, and I thanked him.

Moderna thinks he's hers. He's not, he isn't anybody's. He doesn't want to marry. I quite sympathise. Lots of young men are like that. That's why he gets on so well with me, because he's not afraid of my marrying him.

I disapprove of marriage, but I don't mind helping those wretched grown-up girls a little. Poor things, they are so dreadfully helpless! I've heard that burglars always have a small boy about that they shove through keyholes and pantry windows to open places for them. The girls are always shoving me through the larder window, don't you know? I like it. I have a perfect genius for it.

G

Now, see here, to-day—this tea and tennis! It's all
my getting up. On Tuesday night Moderna couldn't
sleep a wink—she says so, but she had a horrid kind of
broken sleep, I heard her—because she was quite sure
that Arthur Deverel had gone home from the picnic
supper, thinking she had got lost in the woods *on purpose* with Mr. Vere. With Mr. Vere! As if anybody
would take the trouble to get lost with him! She knew,
because he had hardly spoken to her at supper, and she
values his good opinion—anybody's good opinion, she
says, but she can't take *me* in. Although she flirts with
him, do you know, I really think she's in love with
him, so I don't mind helping her.

She got me into her bedroom, and shut all the doors
and windows—I wonder she did not stop up the
chimney—and then she cried a little, and would I help
her and be a dear, and make him understand—oh, very,
very delicately—it would ruin her if he ever guessed—
and all that! So I promised to help her if she'd
promise not to tell about Towzer. *That* happened a
month ago, but I've always been anxious about it, and I
was glad to have an opportunity of making it safe. So
I lent her my handkerchief, and said she wasn't to
bother, and I'd take the whole responsibility. She
stopped howling—I really believe she cares for him—
and gave me an old hat and a yard of Valenciennes that
was lying about. Good business!

So next day I rode over to Dunse Court on 'Freckles'
and asked for Arthur Deverel. I can do these things
because I'm not out. He was in the billiard-room. I
just said, " How-de-do," and then—no silly beating

about the bush—that I was quite sure Moderna liked
him a great deal better than Mr. Vere. We all think
poets horrid. He stared a little and said, "Really!"—
it seemed rather as if he hadn't thought of it before.
Perhaps he doesn't want Moderna? Anyhow, I have
put the idea into his head. Then I asked him over to
tea and tennis to-day—all off my own bat, you know—
and here he is, as large as life, and letting all the balls
go through his racquet, because he's looking at Moderna.
Oh, we'll pull it through, I fancy.

William, you fraud, where have you been? You
found a chaffinch's nest? Good heavens! you say you
called me? I don't believe it. You wanted it all to
yourself—I know you.

No, you shall not have any more. Let go! There,
you can eat that one that's fallen, there, on the ant's
nest. I'd rather you had it than the ants, anyway.

Are they quarrelling over there, or is the game over?
Cut along, William, and tell James I want him. James,
more tea—and—more cakes!—we had a little accident
with those last ones.

Oh, here you all are! Game and sette! Who won?
Moderna, I don't believe you have the very haziest idea.
You haven't! Excuse her, Mr. Deverel. There is
some more tea coming. Have some bread and butter,
Tom. Where is the cake, I wonder?

William, you and I'll have a knock-out now, and
show 'em how. Moderna and Mr. Deverel, suppose
you field for us? It's the least you can do. Come on,
William!

XI

IN MODERNA's room at Merrow.   Midnight.   Enter VERONA *en peignoir.*   She whispers.

"Send away Aurélie."

"Vous pouvez vous en aller, Aurélie."

"Aurélie hates going.   She wanted to listen."

"Nonsense.   Well, she's gone.   What is it?"

"Nothing."

"Well, then, it's dreadfully late—hadn't you better let me get to bed."

"How dreadfully unsympathetic you are.   I want to talk about the dinner party."

"Go on then.   Talk about the dinner party."

A PAUSE.   VERONA speaks.

"Did you notice the widow to-night?"

"I always do.   It's good practice."

"She actually contrived to blush."

"How mean!   She ought to leave blushing to us."

"I never can, even when I want to."

"That's the worst of being a girl."

"I wish I was a widow."

"My dear, Mrs. Jenkyn's twenty-six."

"Awful, isn't it?   And yesterday she told poor Tom Lawrence that she would like to be a mother to him."

"Who told you?"

"Tom did.   He wished she wouldn't—he's got a mother of his own at home, he says, and—"

"Tom tells you, does he?"

"He tells me most things."

"Then I think you have the pull of the widow."

"Oh but, Moderna, she is so clever and *rusée.* He says she bores him; but he always ends by going back to her. She knows exactly what to do, and what to say."

"And doesn't say it—looks it instead."

"Anybody can look foolish, but she looks—unutterable things!"

"Why *did* mother ask her to stay here?"

"Well, I suppose as we have taken a country house, we've got to fill it."

"*She* needn't have been asked."

"She makes things go."

"Not for me."

"The world isn't made for girls."

A PAUSE. VERONA resumes.

"Goodness! You *are* crimping it. Is it for the Deverels' picnic?"

"Not particularly for the picnic. I like to look nice always."

"Do you think it will rain?"

"Wind's better."

"Why?"

"It takes *her* fringe out of curl!"

"I hope it will blow a gale, Moderna."

"You donkey."

"Why am I a donkey?"

"You know best."

"You seem to get on with the Prig, Moderna?"

"Who do you mean?"

"Arthur Deverel."

"Who calls him that?"

"Peggy and I do."

"Oh, you do?"

"Well, he's so solemn, we never can make him talk."

"I never have any difficulty."

"Yes, I wish I could let myself go as you do. I freeze people up so."

"They seem to contrive to exist within a hundred miles of you, dear."

"Who contrive to exist?"

"Don't fish."

"I'm not fishing."

"Mrs. Jenkyn makes up to Tom Lawrence a good deal, don't you think?"

"It's a little way she has."

"But I don't fancy he cares very much for her."

"He sat next her at dinner."

"He sat where Mother put him, of course, but he talked most to the woman on his other side."

"Who was it?"

"Oh—a girl!"

"It was me."

"Was it? I never noticed. I say, Verona, I am

tired of the way I do my hair. How would you like it?
—so?"

"No—hateful—doesn't suit you a bit."

"How then?"

"So! No—so! Any way!"

"You *are* unsympathetic."

A PAUSE. VERONA resumes.

"I shall go away now, I think."

"Shall you?"

"Yes, you won't talk."

"Talk about something sensible and I will."

"For heaven's sake, don't get like Arthur Deverel."

"Don't be rude."

"Oh, Moderna, you don't care for the Prig, really?"

"Suppose we drop that silly name."

"You can't alter him. I've heard of a reformed
rake, but of a reformed prig—never! And he plays
tennis abominably. Who asks him here?"

"I don't."

"Then I suppose Peggy does. She's too cheeky for
anything. I say, what will you swop that gown for in
the wardrobe there—second from the end?"

"Make an offer."

"My *vieux rose.*"

"That old deader. Why, it's nearly worn out!"

"I've hardly had it on."

"Ah, but you 'shab' so easily. You would have to
throw in a hat or something to make it fair."

A PAUSE. VERONA speaks.

"Why, you are in bed!"

"Why not? It's very late."

"I suppose I had better go."

"I suppose you had."

"I feel as if I could talk all night."

"Mercy!"

"You *are* cross, Moderna."

"No, only sleepy."

"Good-night, dear."

"Good-night. Mind you shut the door."

A PAUSE. VERONA comes back.

"Mod, wake up, there's an angel, and tell me one thing."

"What?"

"But you must wake up properly, Moderna. It is so important."

"Bother you, Verona! You can have that dress for your wretched old pink, only let me go to sleep, there's a good child."

"It isn't the dress."

"What then? Be quick, I'm just off again."

"Oh, Moderna, wait one minute. Do you—do you think?—is it me or the widow?"

"Neither, I should think."

"Moderna, please, you might be nice."

"I must, I see, if I am ever to go to sleep at all. Well, she's going by the eleven-ten, day after to-morrow, if that's any consolation to you."

" How do you know ? "

" Mother told me ; besides I saw Tom looking out trains for her."

" Oh dear."

" Silly, she's only playing him off against Mr. Deverel."

" Oh dear ! and is she going to take him away from us too ? "

" I'll see to that. Now listen. Tom is going to stay on at the Deverels till Thursday ; and he said to me yesterday didn't I think your eyes the most beautiful eyes in the whole world ? Now, are you content ? "

" Yes, you darling. You are a dear ! You've made me so happy. I'll let you have the Mercury toque as well, if you take the *vieux rose*, it will make it worth while ; and I shall never, *never* forget what a good sister you've been ; and I daresay if you cock it up a bit at the back, and put new velvet— Pooh ! she's asleep ! "

XII

At Mrs. MORTIMER'S dance in Kensington. With the opening bars of the waltz there is a general move among the couples in the conservatory. MODERNA sits motionless, and watches them pass.

MODERNA.

There she goes ! . . . I know her back. . . . No . . . I'm not jealous. . . . I don't hate her, but . . . I wish . . . Is that you, Verona ?

VERONA, leaving her partner for a moment.

I say, Moderna, don't be an idiot. Dance away and

have a good time.   He is absolutely booked for Flossie Rensselaer.

MODERNA.

I don't know what you mean.

VERONA.

There, you are cross—and I left my partner to come and comfort you !

MODERNA.

Comfort !   You may just go away !   (Verona goes.)   That is the worst of sisters.   They find out everything. Here's Flossie now !

Enter FLOSSIE RENSSELAER.

FLOSSIE.

What are you sitting here alone for, Moderna mia ? Have you not got a partner ?

MODERNA.

Don't be silly, of course I have got a partner.

FLOSSIE.

Well then, don't sit away here where he can't possibly find you.   It looks odd.   Ta-ta !   (Goes on.)

MODERNA.

I suppose it does.   I'll go back.   No, stop, here is my partner !   Is that you, Billy ?   (To BILLY DANVERS, who comes stumbling out into the conservatory.)

BILLY.

Flossie told me I should find you here.

MODERNA.

Kind, considerate Flossie! Well, come and sit down.
I don't want to dance.

BILLY.

I'm sure I don't. It's awfully hot. I'd rather talk to
you than dance, any day.

MODERNA, smiling.

Do I dance so badly then?

BILLY.

Don't be silly, you are a ripping good partner. But
sometimes a fellow feels disinclined—

MODERNA.

Disinclined to prattle? I know. I'm not much at
talking myself to-night.

BILLY.

Yes, you are pale. You do too much. It's that blessed
"Girl's Friendly" you go to. What do girls want to
fag for? But still, I like you anyway, Mod, you are
so soothing. Soothe me!

MODERNA.

You look very nice. Will that do? By the light of
one Chinese lantern I see you are wearing something
very superb in button-holes.

BILLY.

Rather big, don't you think? It isn't mine, either. It was Arthur Deverel's. He gave it me.

MODERNA.

Let me look?

BILLY.

Hands off! I should never get it back again. You may smell it on the tree. I am not going to give it to you.

MODERNA, nervously.

You very cheeky boy! You don't suppose I really want your horrid cabbage of a flower, do you?

BILLY.

Now you've left off being soothing! Everybody is hateful to-night. . . .

[MODERNA.

Who have you been dancing with? Flossie?

BILLY.

No, thank you, I don't care to halve dances with Deverel.

MODERNA.

Not Flossie? Well, who then? (Wearily.) I insist upon knowing.

BILLY.

Nobody, I tell you. Girls always think a fellow must be in love with some one. I am not going to fall in love *any more* till I have passed my exam. Life is far too serious for that sort of humbug.

MODERNA.

Ah, but you will have to make a special study of that sort of humbug when you go in for being a diplomat. It is part of your duty to flirt and make love prettily.

BILLY, with conviction.

Oh, I think I can manage that.   But I consider falling in love—really—awful rot, don't you?   I mean to steer clear of all that bother, as yet.   I get on very well.   I am not in love with any one, not *even* with you.

MODERNA, bitterly.

It's very easy not to be in love with me.

BILLY, politely.

Not at all.   It takes me all my time, I assure you.   If anything, you're not old enough.

MODERNA.

Oh, Billy, how funny you are !   Try Flossie.

BILLY.

Is she older than you ?

MODERNA, repentant.

I don't know, I'm sure.

BILLY.

And besides I shouldn't like to go and cut old Deverel out.

MODERNA.

Is Mr. Deverel—?

BILLY.

Well, just look at them! They are inseparable, and
they don't dance—they talk, and Flossie looks quite
serious, for her! Oh, it's a settled affair, you bet, and
we shall all hear of it to-morrow.

MODERNA.

But . . . I always thought . . . I understood that she was
engaged to his brother Fred. Last autumn at Merrow—

BILLY.

I know. But they had a split; things went wrong somehow. Personally I prefer Fred to Arthur, Arthur's such
a prig. I can't think what the saintly Arthur sees in
Flossie. She's awful sport—but—

MODERNA.

Hush!

BILLY.

Oh, she's not a bad sort, really, only a bit flighty. I've
got a note here, she shoved into my hand in the Lancers.
Shall I show it to you?

MODERNA, leaning forward.

Is it—? You ought not to—I suppose. (With sudden fury.)
I'll never speak to you again if you do.

BILLY.

Of course I shan't—I was only "ragging." It's nothing, only to ask me to let her off three dances she had promised me. She wanted them for Deverel, I suppose.

MODERNA, interrogatively.

She is just the kind of girl who appeals to men—

BILLY.

Yes, she's always appealing and making eyes. Personally I hate it. We all think Deverel an infernal fool. But he's gone too far now to draw back. The Deverels are all awfully punctilious and all that. It will come off to-night. Look here, I'll bet you—I'll bet you anything it comes off to-night. I can find out. I've watched them. Do lay me something on it!

MODERNA.

But then I shall have to bet that it will not come off, and I know it will.

BILLY.

Do it for the sake of argument, as neither of us care twopence either way. Not but what old Deverel's a good sort, a bit of a prig and all that, but I like him.

MODERNA.

I wonder why.

BILLY.

Oh, why do men take to each other? Besides, don't you be mean; at Merrow you and Arthur were rather pals, if I recollect. I'm sorry the American girl has got him.   He's too good for her.   (Meditatively.)   Perhaps her money may have something to do with it.   He wants to go into Parliament, I know.

MODERNA, suddenly.

Have you got the next dance ?

BILLY.

No, 'gave it away.   Why ?   Want to cut it ?

MODERNA.

Yes.

BILLY, anxiously.

Whose is it ?

MODERNA, laughing.

Billy, you are presuming on our intimacy.   Remember I am a young lady who has been out three seasons, and you are a little boy I can use to cut dances with, but I am not bound to give names to you.

BILLY.

I am sorry for him, poor beggar, whoever he is !   You look so nice to-night; you are not pale now, but so red —so red. . . .   I say, there is that rattling good polka *Cut and Run !*   Oh, I can't miss that !

MODERNA.

Of course not.   Run along.   I'll wait here.   (Leans back.)

BILLY.

Really leave you here ?   (Going.)   By the way, what is our bet to be ?

MODERNA.

I don't know.   Anything !   Your buttonhole ?

. .   BILLY.

Aha, you did want it !   I say, Mod, I've a great mind
to stay and see who it is you want to shirk ?

MODERNA.

If you don't cut and run at once I'll never speak to you
again !   All right.   I won't forget the bet.

Exit BILLY.   Enter ARTHUR DEVEREL.

DEVEREL, shortly.

Our dance !   Come and see the night-flowering Cereus
in the hothouse at the bottom of the garden.

MODERNA, rather stiffly.

Isn't it rather cold ?

DEVEREL.

Excuse me, I had thought of that.   Isn't this your wrap?
I fetched it out of the cloakroom for you.   I noticed it
particularly as you came in.   Let us go and look at this
fabulous flower.   Every one has been but me, and I
waited till I could go with you.   I am glad to say I
have done all my duty dances.

MODERNA.

Why, you were dancing with Miss Rensselaer, Mr.
Deverel ?

H

DEVEREL.

Yes, she's going to marry my brother Fred after all.   I
have pulled it straight.   He was so miserable about her.
You have no idea how worried I've been all these
months.   I have had no time to attend to my own
concerns.   Come !   (He puts the wrap carefully round her.   They go.)

*   *   *   *   *

Half an hour later.   They meet BILLY DANVERS and VERONA in the
supper-room.

MODERNA.

Is there any room in here, Billy ?

BILLY.

Yes, Verona and I wiH make room for you.   (Looks at her.
I say, Mod, will you have the buttonhole ?

MODERNA, softly.

Yes, dear boy.

*   *   *   *   *

FROM *MODERNA'S DIARY.*

May 28*th.*—I have told him all.   I hated doing it.   He
didn't mind as much as I expected.   He said Captain
Jekyll had behaved very well.   I told him that Captain
Jekyll married Cissy Riddell six months ago, so I hadn't
done *her* any harm, at any rate.   I am so glad I confessed.   I am quite happy.   How could I have been
jealous—and of Flossie Rensselaer too !   It seems
incredible !   Arthur doesn't think her good form, I
know, though he can't speak out, as she is going to be
his sister-in-law—and mine ! . . .

XIII

On the slope of PICCADILLY on a spring morning.

DEVEREL.

Well, and what did my little Moderna do with herself all yesterday?

MODERNA.

Let me see, Arthur. . . . Well, I had rather a time of it yesterday. William has got his exeat and expects me to be a perfect slave to him—and of course I am—and then I went to lunch with your sainted mother—

DEVEREL, mildly.

My what?

MODERNA.

I beg pardon; Lady Deverel. . . . It was rather an ordeal. . . . I kept hoping you would come in.

DEVEREL, tenderly.

Did you? I wish, dear, you got on better with my mother. She might be of use to you in so many ways if—

MODERNA.

But I *do* like her! I think she's a dear old thing! And your sister is ripping! Oh, I beg your pardon! . . . I seem to be always begging your pardon, Arthur. When William is up from Eton I always get rather slangy. But don't you believe your mother and I don't get on, for we do. She asked me to play to her, and I did— an air with variations—old style! It was rather more modern than they thought. Guess what?

DEVEREL.

I cannot tell.   What are the things girls play now?

MODERNA, laughing.

It wasn't "The Maiden's Prayer," at any rate.   Listen!
It was "*The poor girl didn't know, you know.*"   A lovely
air, and I invented the variations!   They never even
guessed.

DEVEREL, drily.

They wouldn't.   Don't you think, dear, it was rather—

MODERNA, wilfully.

Rather. what?   Why, Maude Valerie White did "*'E
dunno where 'e are* " for us the other day as a fugue.

DEVEREL, reconciled.

It was clever of you, dear.   Why are we stopping?

MODERNA, earnestly surveying the posters on a hoarding.

How pretty that dancing girl is!   I wonder who drew
her?

DEVEREL.

For heaven's sake, don't stop before a hoarding.

MODERNA.

All right, come on!   When we are married, Arthur,
shan't we go to one of those places?

DEVEREL.

What places?   Music halls?   My dear child, they are
so deplorably dull.

MODERNA, aggrieved.

I know, that is what all the married women say, who have been once, and want to persuade their innocent sisters that it is sour grapes. Why Flossie Deverel, your own sister-in-law, went the other day, and she and Fred pinned the curtains forward with her bonnet-pin, and looked through, and had a perfectly lovely time.

DEVEREL, sententiously.

Please don't take my sister-in-law as your model. I had rather you didn't, and I don't think Americanisms sound well in the mouth of a lovely English girl.

MODERNA.

I must say, Arthur, that when you do pay one a compliment, you lay it on with a trowel!... But I do really mean to learn skirt-dancing. Don't you think I could do it rather well? I am not a bit stiff, I can twist any way. (Looks as if she were going to begin that very minute.)

DEVEREL, fondly.

You shall, dear, and dance it for me, your husband, alone.

MODERNA, with modified enthusiasm.

Ah! (Walks on in silence. A fire-engine rattles by.) Oh, look, Arthur, it's going down there! Let's go and see the fire. We must!...

DEVEREL.

But, dearest, it is quite out of the question. There will be an awful crowd.

MODERNA.

Of course, that's half the fun. Do let's. (To a small boy.)
Tell me the way to the fire?

THE BOY.

Only a chimbly in Montpelier Square, Miss.   It's out,
nearly.

DEVEREL.

Please, Moderna, don't speak to little boys in the street.
Come along, let's turn into the Gardens.

MODERNA, submissively.

All right, dear.   (Makes a sudden dive between three converging omni-
buses. He joins her on the opposite side.)

MODERNA.

I love getting right under the horses' noses, don't you?
It's so exciting!

DEVEREL.

Yes, dear, only my trousers are covered with mud.

MODERNA.

Oh, come along, no one will look at you.   (They enter the
Gardens. MODERNA picks budding horse-chestnut leaves and strips them with
her teeth.)

DEVEREL.

Don't dear, it will make your teeth quite green.   (They
appropriate two chairs under a tree. DEVEREL gazes tenderly at MODERNA,
who has obediently left off eating green leaves and sits back, looking a little bored.)

DEVEREL.

Now, darling, let us talk seriously. That pretty little head must make plans, and be business-like sometimes. I should like—that day we know of—

MODERNA.

Why can't you say wedding-day right out?

DEVEREL.

The date of our marriage fixed, so that I could arrange some nice place to go where I could have you all to myself.

MODERNA, eagerly.

I know where *I* should like to go.

DEVEREL.

Where? Scotland? Norway? It used to be quiet there, but lately it has been overrun with tourists.

MODERNA.

Delightful! Still, I had rather go to Paris. Flossie and Fred did.

DEVEREL.

I'm sick to death of Paris! If you only knew how—

MODERNA.

But *I'm* not, and I *don't* know. (Piteously.) I want to go to the theatres, and the Palais Royal farces, and the Cafés, and the Quartier Latin, and the Chaumière—

DEVEREL, fondly.

Silly little thing ! The Chaumière died long before you were born.

MODERNA.

One reads of it in *The Newcomes*. And there is sure to be something new that corresponds to it ?

DEVEREL, drily.

No doubt—but I couldn't take my pearl there.

A Pause.

DEVEREL.

And what other dreadful things do you want to do when you are married ?

MODERNA.

Heaps of things ! Read French novels—all those I may not read now.

DEVEREL, indulgently.

I daresay I could look you out some French books that you *might* read now.

MODERNA, rudely.

I know—like the French shelf in the school library. *Recit d'une Sœur*, and the *Romance of an Idiotic Young Man*, or whatever it is ? I want to read Droz, and De Maupassant, and Zola, and—

DEVEREL, with violence.

I had rather my wife lay dead at my feet than that she should read Zola !

MODERNA, sweetly.

Then I won't.   You can tell me all the plots yourself.

DEVEREL.

Heaven forbid!   You don't seem to understand, dearest
—I want to preserve you, my flower, my white lily, as you,
are ; to enfold you with my love, to protect, to cherish
you, and not let anything painful or ugly or disagreeable
come near you, my sweet, if I can help it.   I always
think of that beautiful observation of Shakespeare's—

> " He might not even let the winds of Heaven
> Visit her face too roughly."

MODERNA, a little impressed.

Arthur, dear, it's very pretty, but I enjoy the winds of
heaven, and (laughing), to be prosaic, I don't chap easily.
I'm awfully strong.   Feel my biceps. . . .

DEVEREL.

You oughtn't to have a biceps.

MODERNA.

No biceps, no arm, no wrist, no finger to put your pretty
engagement ring on !   Feel, all the same.   Even William
says it is fine—for a girl.   (He touches her arm gingerly, with an eye
to an old gentleman who is feeding the ducks. MODERNA takes off her glove
and examines her engagement ring.)

DEVEREL.

What pretty filbert nails you have !   There is such dis-
tinction about them.   I don't think I could have fallen
in love with a woman who had square nails.

MODERNA, wilfully.

I bite them.

DEVEREL.

Naughty little thing! We must cure you of that (fondly), then you will be quite perfect.   I shall have the sweetest and prettiest woman in England for my wife.

MODERNA, bitterly.

Oh yes, people like you always have everything perfect. Perfect house!   Perfect wines!   Perfect wife—

DEVEREL, mildly.

Yes, dear, do you know, I always think that a man's wife, as it were, explains him.

MODERNA.

Then it is to be my mission in life to explain you!   But who is going to explain *me* ?   (DEVEREL fails to find any point in her remark, but is vaguely distressed. He takes her hand, which she draws away pettishly.)

MODERNA.

Don't !

DEVEREL.

Why not ?

MODERNA.

Somebody might be looking out of a window in the Palace, and see you.

DEVEREL, with discernment.

Have I said anything to vex you, darling ?

MODERNA.

No . . . yes . . . you can't help it . . . but you talk so . . .
foolishly . . . so narrowly.   You don't seem to see that
a woman has a soul to save as well as a man ; a personality she ought to develop ; a life to live—

DEVEREL, sadly.

Ah, dear, I see that you too have got hold of that
dreadful modern jargon of repressed personalities and
baulked vocations, that leads eventually to public plat-
forms and "Women's Rights," and monstrous develop-
ments of that kind.   You have been reading Ibsen.   If
women would only be content to stay in the niche that
Providence intended for them !   Dearest, don't you see
that a man like me is, or ought to be, able to satisfy
every yearning of a woman's nature, sympathise with all
the aspirations of her being, and comprise them in his,
as the greater includes the less.   She lives in his life, as
it were, and her lighter nature finds its expression in
his deeper one. . . .

MODERNA, with sarcasm.

Arthur, you quite overwhelm me with your eloquence.
The case has never been put so clearly to me before.

DEVEREL.

You see my point, don't you, dear ?   You know I hold
such very chivalrous views about women.   They are so
infinitely pathetic to me, in their gentle fragile depend-
ence.   Don't you know Tennyson says—
      " Men are God's trees, and women are His flowers."

MODERNA.

Pshaw! "Half-hours with the Poets." There are
dozens of quotations like that. Men wrote them, of
course. "The sturdy oak and the clinging vine."
(Shortly.)   I don't want to cling.

DEVEREL.

It's a law of nature. Women are bound to be dependent.
You can't help your dear little selves. And think how
beautiful an arrangement it is ! Man goes out and toils
in the heat and labour of the day, and comes home in
the evening, weary and worn out, and finds his wife, in
her soft warm nest, waiting for him. . . .

MODERNA, flippantly.

In her boudoir, in a lovely tea-gown, pouring out tea for
half a dozen men who are calling, and who glare—

DEVEREL, revolted.

Moderna !

MODERNA.

It's no good, dear.   I'm cross.   Let's go home.

DEVEREL.   .

But—!

MODERNA.

Yes, it's going to rain.   These spring mornings are so
treacherous.

DEVEREL.

You surely don't mind a shower ?

MODERNA.

Yes, I might melt.   Fragile, with care !   (Rises.)

DEVEREL.

Well, if you will ?   Take my arm then.

˙ MODERNA.

No, thank you . . . dear.

AT THE PARK GATES.

MODERNA.

Dear, I'm not at all nice to-day, and I think you had better not come back to lunch.   William is there— and I'm going to have a headache, and a real bad temper in my own room, and I'm going to dine at the Mortimers in the evening.   (Hails a 'bus.)   Best for you and best for me.   Good-bye.   You may come and dine to-morrow—unless you hear.   (The omnibus stops.)

DEVEREL, surprised.

Did you hail it ?   (She nods and gathers up her skirts.)   Darling, when you are mine you shall never go in an omnibus !

MODERNA.

Till then—!   (Gets in.)   Good-bye.

UNSPOKEN THOUGHTS.

His.

Dear little girl !   But she needs an immense amount of breaking in.   My Mother—

Hers.

Love in a cottage is all very well, but love in a band-box— I should die ! I shall have to find some way out of this. . . .

XIV

1

Dearest—Why were you not at my mother's reception to-day ? I will go to you at three to-morrow.—Yours always,   A. D.

2

Dearest—No, don't come at three.   Come at four.— Yours always,   M. M.

3

Dearest—I called at four precisely, and you had gone out.   I ascertained.   How about Thursday. — Yours always,   A. D.

4

Dear Arthur.—I beg your pardon, but I did not go out till five minutes past four.   I am so sorry. — In haste, yours,   M. M.

P.S.—I have an engagement on Thursday.

5

My dear Moderna—When may I come, then ?   I have so much to say.   Friday ?—Yours,   A.

6

Dear Arthur—No, not Friday. I have to go to my cookery class in the morning, and to my gymnasium in the afternoon. I shall be too tired to do anything after. Saturday I go to Eton to see William, and a dinner in the evening; Sunday I am going to the Temple Church with Billy Danvers, and in the afternoon to a Bohemian tea-party that I don't want to miss. It is no use my offering to take you—you would hate it. Don't trouble to send me flowers for to-night. I've left off wearing them, it's not fashionable; besides it spoils the fronts of one's gowns so.—Yours,   M. MASKELYNE.

7

My dearest Moderna—Do you realise that it is a whole week since I have seen you, and you keep putting me off. I begin to think there is something behind. Write by the next post.—Yours always, dear Moderna,

ARTHUR DEVEREL.

.8

Well, then, dear Arthur, if you will have it, there is. I have been meaning to tell you for a long time, but you are always so nice that it is difficult to be disagreeable to you. But I have been thinking—don't you guess what I am coming to when I begin like that? Oh, I wish you *would* guess, and save me the pain of telling you. You must see it yourself, dear Arthur, you must see that we are not really in sympathy with each other. We must not marry. I should never make you

happy — or you me.   That would be my fault, not
yours.   Do be kind and sensible, and not want me to
explain.   I *can't* explain—it's inexplicable, the divergence
between us.   Put it this way,—say I am horrid and you
are nice ; and congratulate yourself on having been
saved from a wife who would make you quite miserable.

I am going away for a little.   When I come back,
come and see me, and let us be friends, but don't come
now.   I could not explain it to you if you did—I can't
explain it to myself—but I *know* we should be miserable
together,   M. M.

9

If it is as you say, I must accept your decision, only
I *must* hear it from your own lips.   I will come to-
morrow evening at nine,   A. D.

PEGGY, reading the last.

They always want to hear it from one's own disagreeable
lips !   So silly !   Did you tell him you were dining
out ?

MODERNA.

Yes.   He must have forgotten.

PEGGY.

You *can't* be so horrid as to go ?

MODERNA.

I am not going to play Mrs. Mortimer false because
Arthur can't take No for an answer.   Oh, why can't he

understand, and stay away?   It's so *dreadfully* unsympathetic and stupid of him.   (Wails.)

PEGGY.

That's just what you complain of in him, isn't it?

MODERNA.

Yes.   Why can't he see that I don't want a scene, that I can't explain or give a reason.   I *have* no reason—no tangible reason.

PEGGY.

Except that you think you are too good for him.

MODERNA.

I *don't.*   How can you say such things?   I wish I hadn't told you.

PEGGY.

Well, you think you are different to other people; that there is something distinctive about you—more character, and all that.   I don't know what it is, but—

MODERNA.

Then you think me conceited?

PEGGY.

Oh no, I don't think you have anything to be conceited about—really.   Look here, he means to-night, and it's six now.   What are you going to do about Arthur?   Must you really jilt him?

I

MODERNA.

Is it really jilting? I suppose it is. Well, it must be given out that he has jilted me.

PEGGY.

No, *that* I will not allow. I shall tell every one the version I mean them to accept. Look here, Arthur's a prig, I know—I always said so; but must you—can't you put up with him—can't you mould him? It's so much nicer to have the eldest engaged and married, so as to—

MODERNA.

I can't spoil my whole life and his, for the sake of taking my younger sisters out. Verona must do it, or you. I'm going to be a bachelor.

PEGGY, resignedly.

Or an obstinate idiot. . . . Well, he must be told—somehow. How do you mean to do it?

MODERNA, hesitating.

Don't you think I might let him come, and—

PEGGY.

And then you would make *me* see him. Oh, you coward !

MODERNA, with scorn.

You—you would take the skin off anybody with your tongue ! No, I meant Mother . . . she might explain to him . . .

PEGGY.

She'd muddle it!

MODERNA, sharply.

She would do it like a lady at any rate, and that's the point. All the better if she does muddle him a little. I don't want to hurt his feelings by explaining, so long as he knows I don't want to be engaged any more! Mother must tell him that I am not going to marry; that I think a woman much happier not married; that I think men, when one knows them, are odious—

PEGGY, drily.

He will like that! (Curiously.)   I say, Moderna, does he ever kiss you?

MODERNA.

Yes . . . I suppose so. . . .

PEGGY.

And do you like it?

MODERNA, impatiently.

I never think about it. It doesn't count. It's one of the formalities of being engaged. . . . I hate being engaged. I was never meant to be engaged. I wish I could have been a boy, with a cropped head, and a sword, and a sash tied on one side, and flirt desperately with every woman I met, and make her miserable—like a man. It must be delightful to choose, instead of being chosen—to "run around," as Flossie Deverel says, and do everything, and go everywhere, and "love and ride away." . . . !

PEGGY, carried away.

It's a good thing you are not a boy.   What a villain you
would be!

MODERNA.

Still, as a mere wretched girl, I don't see why I shouldn't
have a very good time.   I do so want to see the world,
and make my own mistakes, and be accountable to
nobody. . . . ·

PEGGY.

A kind of Peregrina Pickle! I see.   You will get into
some awful muddle, I know, if you begin like this.
You frighten me, positively.   (Shudders.)

MODERNA.

Don't be affected, Peggy.   Whatever I do, I shall hurt
nobody but myself.   Whereas, if I had a husband, I
assure you I should be quite idiotically careful—not to
give him away.   I should feel I was responsible for his
peace of mind.   I should not like to hurt his vanity by
being horrid and reckless and bad form.   Just fancy
having the honour of the Deverels to take care of!   But
now as I am, unattached. . . .

PEGGY.

What awful rot!   You can disgrace your family!   Every
fast thing you do, people will say how badly mother
brought you up!   *I* should hate to have a larky sister.
It would injure my prospects.   No, it won't do.   I
have only been out two years, but I am practical; and

I notice things.   You never do, you are too harum-
scarum and artistic.   It's all very well when you are
young to be unconventional; people laugh *with* you,
and think its only artlessness and youthful spirits; but
by and by, when you are thirty and "stale and flat and
unprofitable,"—I heard Billy Danvers say that of Lady
Dean the other day,—people will laugh *at* you, and that
isn't so nice.   Now, while you are young and pretty—

MODERNA, laughing.

I thought you said just now that I had nothing to be
conceited about?

PEGGY, disconcerted.

You look rather nice in that frock.   It makes your
waist quite small—it really does.   Come along and
dress.

Exeunt

XV

THE same evening.   Twelve o'clock.   MODERNA enters in her white
dress and cloak, to find PEGGY in bed.   She gently touches her on the
shoulder.

MODERNA, eagerly.

It's me! . . . Well, what happened?

PEGGY.

Wait till I wake up!   (Sits up in bed.)   Well . . . he came!

MODERNA.

Cross?

PEGGY.

I didn't see the beginnings of him. I was out on the balcony, "inhaling the vernal airs of spring"; but when he was announced I left off inhaling them, and listened instead to what was going on inside.

MODERNA.

Listened?

PEGGY.

I only mean Arthur didn't see me. Listening from a balcony is the same as reading a post-card—everybody does it.

MODERNA.

I always notice post-cards take three times as long as a letter to travel from the front door to the drawing-room.

PEGGY.

Don't interrupt me if you want to hear. Mother received him—she looked awfully dignified and respectable. "Out, is she?" was the first thing I heard. Then mother mumbled something—I felt so inclined to shout "Speak up!"—and he said, "I assure you, Mrs. Maskelyne, I never dreamt of this . . ." What a hypocrite you must have been, Moderna!

MODERNA.

If he hadn't been so conceited he would have guessed. Why, every time he took my hand—I wanted him to

sometimes—and then when he did, I felt I'd rather not
—oh, so much rather! He pretended so hard to be
interested in the things I was interested in—as if I was
such a fool that I could not find out he was pretending.
And when once we were married, he was going to shut
me up in a band-box! He's hopelessly conventional.
Now, I like dress and compliments and drawing-rooms,
and all that, well enough, but I wanted to go down into
the arena and fight with beasts, and he would never
have let me.

PEGGY.

As long as he offered to fight them for you, I don't
see—

MODERNA.

I was to sit behind a lattice, like a Queen at a tourna-
ment . . . see the world through his eyes . . .

PEGGY.

Such fishy eyes too! They have no expression. . . .
Well, then mother said, "My daughter is very young
for her age, she really knows nothing of the world—and
her own good. She is full of fancies, dear child. I
wish you had waited a little while before proposing."

MODERNA.

Oh dear, that isn't at all the line I meant her to take!

PEGGY.

Then he said—he is always dragging Lady Deverel in
—" My mother and Almeria will be so distressed. . . ."

MODERNA.

That's not true. They'll be glad. They are awfully
well-bred, and they mean to treat me properly ; but they
regard me with tolerance, tempered with aversion.

PEGGY.

"So am I distressed," Mother said, "at the turn things
have taken "—and she "didn't know what to do ; you
were so headstrong, she never ventured to interfere with
you "—

MODERNA.

Doesn't she ? That is one of the reasons I wanted to
get married—

PEGGY.

Nonsense, you were in love with Arthur ! She "could
do nothing at present, but she hoped that it might all
come right in the end . . . if Arthur would go away for
a little " . . .

MODERNA, furious.

In short, she told him he might "call again !" (Dashes
across the room to a writing-table.) She bade him hope—she
hasn't disillusioned him a bit—he just thinks it is a mere
girlish caprice. He'll send me alternate bouquets and
boxes of bonbons for a month, and then expect to come
back and find a repentant—oh, I must write to-night !

PEGGY.

Wait a bit. You needn't write. He is quite disillusioned now.

MODERNA.

What do you mean ?

PEGGY.

I mean that when I saw how things were going, I thought
it was time to put in my little, but by no means con-
temptible, oar. I consider I made the engagement—
don't you recollect that summer at Merrow?—and it
was my business to unmake it. So I walked right to
the other end of the balcony and then rustled back, and
came in airily and remarked that it was getting cold. . . .

MODERNA.

Peggy, you fraud !

PEGGY.

I know—for you ! I just tipped Mother the wink—not
one of your ponderous ones, but a dear little delicate
wink that she caught at once—and in five minutes she
had neuralgia enough to go upstairs for her salts, and
wit enough to stay there.

MODERNA.

Well, and then ?

PEGGY.

He sat still, and looked expectant. I sat down, and I
said, " Very rude of my little sister to go out to-night,
wasn't it ? But she always does what she likes—she
never troubles to consider anybody's feelings." . . .

MODERNA.

Really, Peggy !

PEGGY.

Disillusioning him, you know. " Did she know I was
coming ? " he asked fiercely. " I imagined she hadn't

got my note." "Got it fast enough," I said, "but she wanted to go to the Mortimers, and she went." He said, "I can't believe in such want of feeling"—I'm not sure he didn't say proper feeling—"she knew I had to see her on a matter of urgent importance— "

MODERNA.

I *begged* him not to try and see me !

PEGGY.

I said so. I said you hated scenes, and wanted it all to pass off with the least possible wear and tear to your own nerves. "She is very hard," I said; "didn't you find her so?" "Very reserved, very simple, very un-sophisticated," he said—how I laughed inside !—"but I always thought that would pass off, after— "

MODERNA, scornfully.

When he had *un*sophisticated me by contact with his "larger nature." . . . Oh, I know it all. . . .

PEGGY.

Then he said, "I was fool enough to imagine she cared for me."

MODERNA.

I did. I was dreadfully in love with him once. I can't understand. . . . I knew no better, I suppose.

PEGGY, severely.

It is a great pity you know better now. Look at the trouble you give ! . . . So then I told him that he had never understood you . . . you had all sorts of dreadful theories. . . . I gave him a general idea of them, and he didn't like it at all. He kept saying, "I should never have thought—" And I told him you had all sorts of bad habits, that you were lazy and unpunctual and untidy and bad-tempered and tiresome—he will think that I am jealous of you, but never mind. I don't care what he thinks of me, I wouldn't marry him for worlds, there's absolutely nothing in him but good breeding.

MODERNA.

Well, but you needn't have said I was bad-tempered. I am not.

PEGGY.

Not if you get all your own way. Besides, if one wants to disillusion anybody one can't pitch it too strong, and I flatter myself I've done it thoroughly. He looked as if he had never taken in so many new ideas in so short a time in his life.

MODERNA.

Well, I suppose I am obliged to you, dear, but . . . did he express no regret whatever?

PEGGY.

Oh yes, of course, conventionally; but I think he felt as if he had escaped marrying a sort of domestic earthquake—a kind of family typhoon.—

MODERNA.

And didn't he ask if there was some one else?

PEGGY.

I really can't remember.   You needn't feel any remorse,
I assure you ; he is not going either to die or to drop us ;
he is going away for a time, and then coming to call as
if nothing had happened.   I made him promise not to
write to you, or interfere with you in *any way*.   He
accepts your verdict as final.   Now go away and let me
go to sleep, there's a good girl. . . .

MODERNA, wearily.

Will you just unhook me first ?   (Pensively.)   He never
really cared for me or he couldn't have taken it so
calmly.   Why, even I, who don't love him, can't—I
am quite nervous.

PEGGY.

You're nervous because you have taken the plunge.

MODERNA.

Plunge into what ?

PEGGY.

Into old maidenhood, I'm afraid.   I don't know who is
going to marry such a cantankerous girl !   It's a bad
business.   I shall write and tell Edward all about it
to-morrow.

MODERNA, fiercely.

Edward !   Why ?

PEGGY.

Because he charged me, when he went away, to be the
gazette of the Maskelyne family, and tell him all the
news—and this is a very important event.

MODERNA.

I forbid you to mention it to him, do you hear? Let him find it out! Good-night. . . . I suppose I ought to thank you. . . .

XVI

In BILLY DANVERS' rooms in the Temple.

MODERNA.

Quick, Peggy will be here in a moment! She's letting Mr. Darcy show her the church. I said I was tired of the Templar tombs and I would come up here, and put your kettle on for you.

BILLY.

You oughtn't to come here alone, you know.

MODERNA.

What does it matter? It's only you! I've known you since you were so high. (Indicating a certain vague level.) I told Peggy she was to spin it out as long as she could, so we should have time to read Father's answer to my letter. Quick! Has he answered it?

BILLY.

I declare, I've been too lazy to look. There the letters are, on the mantelpiece, the accumulation of three days! I've not been here since I saw you.

MODERNA.

Open them, quick, before the others come. I'll put the kettle on for you. Where is the silly thing?

BILLY.

Over there. It's all ready.

MODERNA.

Get on, open them! What a pile! Miss out the bills.

BILLY, taking a sheaf of letters off the mantelshelf.

It's a wise man knows a bill when he sees one. Here, I'm too lazy, you shall open them.

MODERNA.

Never!—I should hate to. I should be so afraid of coming on pink scented ones, and silver monograms, and all that sort of thing. . . .

BILLY, delighted.

Not many of those, I think. Bill . . . bill. . . . What name did you write to your father under?

MODERNA.

Maude Grey. It sounds convincing, doesn't it?

BILLY.

About as convincing as Miss Clara Montague and Miss Daisy Montgomery. He most likely won't answer at all.

MODERNA.

Oh, you don't know Father. He delights in being given
an opportunity of snubbing some one, and I have the
greatest opinion of his judgment, really. He won't
snub my novel unless it deserves it. I daresay it does.
I daresay he'll say I'm to put it in the fire. It's best to
have an unbiassed opinion, isn't it? Go on, why don't
you look for the letter. It *must* be there. It's three
days since I wrote. What is in that big envelope?

BILLY.

Tailor's patterns, I know.

MODERNA, turns the letters over in desperation.

Not this!—not this. . . . What a smell of bad scent!

BILLY, pausing.

That's this one. Look! Isn't it smart?

MODERNA, reads.

"The Sisters Brace (Maud and Topsy) request the
pleasure of Mr. Danvers' and friend's company at a ball, to
be given on the occasion of their benefit on the stage of
the 'Vanities' on Friday 16th." Are you going? Take
me!

BILLY.

Masked?

MODERNA.

I'd manage somehow. Oh, Billy, about Father's letter—
I've gone through them all, and the answer doesn't seem
to be there?

BILLY, taking up the big envelope.

Dear me ! It isn't tailor's patterns, it's a manuscript . . . To Miss Maude Grey, and G. E. M. in the corner. . . .

MODERNA, in great excitement.

Quick ! Open it. Oh, I hope those Templar tombs will hold out a little longer. I don't want Peggy and Mr. Darcy till we have read Father's letter.

BILLY, reads.

" Madam :—I am deeply flattered by your allusions to my literary sagacity, and my European reputation—"

MODERNA.

That fetched him ! I thought it would.

BILLY, reads.

" But I take this opportunity of assuring you that I am the last person in the world to consult with regard to a work of fiction. As a matter of fact I never read any—"

MODERNA.

Oh ! He reviews novels for the *Incorruptible* once a week !

BILLY, reads.

"— I review them. At the same time, I shall be delighted to give you the benefit of my opinion, such as it is. You say, very nicely, that you are not thin-skinned, and that you hope you can bear the truth. You beg that I will not spare it you, however bitter. My dear madam, let me tell you no one knows how thin-skinned they are till they try—or are tried. Having glanced, superficially, at the manuscript in question, it occurs to me that I can be of greater assistance to you in your literary career if I confine my remarks to generalities, and speak with that total absence of knowledge which characterises the mere reviewer. I apprehend—wrongly perhaps—that you are very young and *blasée*; that you think a literary career will be the crowning glory of a well - spent girlhood. So, having exhausted all the amusements proper to your sex, such as bazaars, balls, ambulance classes, tea, tennis, and flirtation, you have at last sported your feminine oak—"

MODERNA.

I wrote it chiefly at Merrow, in the apple tree.

BILLY, reading.

"Laid in a gross of Waverley pens, and a ream of sermon paper, and produced an immortal work—"

MODERNA, nervously.

I begin to think, Billy, that I should like to read this to myself.

BILLY.

No—that's not fair! "Letters Received Here" only on condition the tobacconist—that's me!—reads them too.

MODERNA, resigned.

Go on.

K

BILLY, reading.

"I take it for granted you have found a plot—a good working plot, one that will go on all fours—the more commonplace the better. On the other hand I trust you have not chosen the distressed-governess root, the missing-will root, the *femme-incomprise* root, the rascally-banker root, the fair—false—fatal siren root, or the purloined-letter root. You have had nothing to do, I hope, with courts of justice, smoking rooms, dissecting rooms, the turf, or the stage. You know nothing about them, or if you do, you ought not to—" There, miss! That's what Father would think of the "voyages of discovery" you make me aid and abet you in!

MODERNA.

How can one write a novel without seeing life! Go on.

BILLY, reading.

"If your heart is set on having a marquis for a hero, be brave beyond the manner of women, and drop him a peg lower, make him a viscount or an earl. Avoid dukes and detectives, ladies-maids and lawyers, doctors and the *demi-monde*. They are more trouble than they are worth—". Oh, I say, listen to this!— "Don't describe father, and mother, your elder sister, your maiden aunt, and the curate of the parish. It is a delightful outlet, but is apt to lead to unpleasantness." Have you described them, dear?

MODERNA.

All of them, except the curate of the parish.   I don't
know him.   .

BILLY, reading.

More shame for you.—"Steer clear of your juvenile
recollections.   We have all had them.   Everybody has
robbed the orchard once in his youth, or tied a tin kettle
to a dog's tail—"

MODERNA, indignantly.

I never did anything so commonplace.   Go on.

BILLY, reading.

"Now as to your choice of a heroine.   Be advised.
She need not unite, in her own person, every virtue and
every attraction, human and divine.   Make her like
yourself—" I really think he guesses, Moderna, don't
you?—"she had really better not have fluffy golden
hair, with soft tendrils straying over a white forehead—a
flower-like mouth—eyes in whose depths you can
temporarily lose yourself, or dark lashes lying on a pale
pure cheek, which, as a mere mechanical feat, is impossible "—What about yours ?

MODERNA.

Mine don't, nor do my heroine's.   Go on.

BILLY, reading.

"Don't rush to the other extreme and make her
rather under than over middle height, with eyes of no
particular shade—mouse-coloured hair, and a sallow

complexion.   Stumpy heroines went out with Jane Eyre, and it takes a Becky Sharp to make green eyes go down. As for your hero, you will probably make him like the only man you ever loved, and I don't wish to be personal."—That's as well, isn't it?—"Don't give your villain away at the outset, and spoil all his little plans by endowing him with a dusky complexion, a cat-like tread, sinister eyes, a sardonic mouth, and no belief in anything whatever.   And don't engage all our sympathies for your villainess, in preference to the wishy-washy heroine, by describing her as a rare exotic, with lips like a scarlet thread, dark passionate eyes, an undulating gait, masses of black hair, and no conscience at all"—

MODERNA.

Oh dear, who could publish a novel after this!   I'll burn it.

BILLY, reading.

"Don't let your villain hiss anything, whether vows of love or vengeance, in your heroine's ears.   Don't exhibit 'a strong man in his agony.'   Don't end a chapter 'Their lips met in one long rapturous kiss.' It's stale and it's improper.   Don't let her go erect and tearless to meet her doom, or flash defiance on any number of her traducers"—I agree with all this.   Now come a lot of short sentences.   Can you bear any more?

MODERNA.

Go on.

BILLY, reading.

"Mind your spelling.   Don't over-praise your own sex,

or abuse ours. Don't be long-winded. Don't be snappy. Take out every third word and every second adjective. Don't deal too much in dots, or be lavish of lines, or abuse the useful asterisk. Don't neglect the humble comma."—Just listen how he ends !—"If there's anything left of it after this, take my advice, and don't send it, tied up with blue ribbon, to the first man you meet who has the misfortune to be an editor. I am, dear madam, yours faithfully, Gervaise Maskelyne."— Well, I call that a perfectly brutal performance !

MODERNA.

Oh, I don't care. It's frank. It's clever. I don't think I *shall* send my novel to a publisher. It isn't quite like that, but it's rot. I shall burn it. . . . Here, make the tea ! I see Peggy and Mr. Darcy just crossing the court.

XVII

THE study of GERVAISE MASKELYNE, Professor of Numismatics, Egyptology, Philology, and several other 'ologies. He is seated at his desk. MODERNA half opens the door.

MODERNA.

You sent for me, father ?

GERVAISE MASKELYNE, impatiently.

Come in, for God's sake, come *quite* in. Don't stand rattling the handle of the door in that fashion.

MODERNA.

No, father, I don't want to, for I've got on a preposterous hat, and you'll destroy all my confidence in it.

GERVAISE MASKELYNE, fretfully.

Come in, I tell you.   Take the hat off!

MODERNA.

But, Father, listen.   I haven't a minute.   I'm off to my cookery class, and I only wanted to ask you if you could get tickets for the Royal Institution on Friday night, for me and Mrs. Mortimer.   There is a lecture about Phagocytes I want to hear.

GERVAISE MASKELYNE.

Good Lord!   What do you know of Phagocytes?

MODERNA.

Not much, father, but I like to improve my mind. Besides it's so interesting.   It's like the story of a battle. The powers of Good and Evil, Light and Darkness—

GERVAISE MASKELYNE.

Ormuzd and Ahriman, Indra and Siva, and all the rest of it.   Women always want a romantic basis to their science—don't take it in unless it's popularised.   Lauder Brunton says that "the death of a mouse from anthrax may be compared with the destruction of the Roman Empire by the Barbarians."   There, will that do for you?   Come here and sit down, you have nothing to do, of course.

MODERNA.

Why, father, I told you—

GERVAISE MASKELYNE.

You might look through these numbers of the *Numismatic Review* for me, and see if you can find any mention of the coinage of Cyzicus. Write it down, when you find it, on a slip . . . here . . .

MODERNA.

How do you spell Cyzicus?

GERVAISE MASKELYNE.

Don't worry *me*, child. Look in the dictionary.

MODERNA, goes to a shelf.

How can I when I don't know what letter it begins with even? Never mind. I will go by the light of reason. S.Y., or perhaps it's P.S.Y.? How clever of me! I'll look it out both ways. (Seeks with ardour.)

* * * * *

GERVAISE MASKELYNE.

What a draught you are making, turning pages at that rate? Here, let me see, I'll find it myself. . . .

MODERNA.

Oh, please, father, let me help you *some* way.

GERVAISE MASKELYNE.

You have made rather a mess of it so far. (Drily.) Wait, I had something to say to you, but I can't remember it . . . your mother was saying. . . .

MODERNA.

All right, father dear, keep calm. I'll stay here till you remember, and tidy up your papers a bit.

GERVAISE MASKELYNE.

Eh, what ? . . . (Takes out a pocket-lens and becomes absorbed.)

*   *   *   *   *

MODERNA.

What's all this ?   Edward's writing.   (Reads.)   "*Now hath the lord of earth slain falls the land under the descendants of Ella forward in fight of rule head-stem three princes.*"   What rubbish !

GERVAISE MASKELYNE, almost mechanically.

Which being interpreted means "*Now hath the lord of earth forward in fight, head-stem slain three princes. The land falls under the rule of Ella.*"

MODERNA.

It doesn't make much sense either way.

GERVAISE MASKELYNE.

That involution of words is the constant practice of the Skalds.   It sometimes makes Scandinavian verse highly unintelligible.   How I wish I had Edward here to keep me up in it all.   How did you stumble on those notes of his ?   I lost them a hundred years ago.

MODERNA.

Tidying, father.

GERVAISE MASKELYNE.

Tidying! Mixing! Confusing! Good heavens, a woman in a study is as bad as a cow in a garden. Confound it! D—m!...

MODERNA, very seriously.

Father, what religion are you?

GERVAISE MASKELYNE, sharply.

Is that a question for a nineteenth-century child to ask?

MODERNA.

Because I had a long argument with Billy Danvers yesterday. He was trying to convert me to be a Roman Catholic—he's going to be one, he says it is such a comfortable religion and saves so much time; and I said no, I would stick to the faith of my fathers —that sounds well, don't you think?—and then he laughed, and said it would puzzle any one to find out the religion of *my* father. So I began to think about it. . . .

GERVAISE MASKELYNE.

And at what conclusion did you arrive, most sapient of modern maidens?

MODERNA.

Well, *I think* you are an agnostic, at any rate, because you said, only yesterday, *à propos* of being invited to brush your hat before you went out, that you "didn't believe in a next world, and didn't want to be plagued in this."

GERVAISE MASKELYNE, suavely.

You've forgotten to put the stopper back in the ink-
bottle. . . .

A Pause.

MODERNA.

Well, father, if I cannot do anything more for you—?
(Aside.)   They will have got to the Chaud-froid of
Chicken by now . . . Oh dear !

GERVAISE MASKELYNE.

Yes, you can.   Look out Lawrence in the County
Families for me.

MODERNA.

Lawrence with a *w* ?   What do you care about people's
families ?

GERVAISE MASKELYNE, solemnly.

A father has duties.   What are the arms of the family
of Lawrence ?

MODERNA.

I can't quite tell, . . . it looks like three sparrows
running up an incline.

GERVAISE MASKELYNE.

Good God, child !   Three martlets on a bend.

MODERNA.

How was I to know ?

GERVAISE MASKELYNE.

Don't you know heraldry ?

MODERNA, laughing.

No, father.   It's your fault, you've never taught me either heraldry or religion.

GERVAISE MASKELYNE.

I haven't time.   (Sadly.)   I've never had time.

MODERNA.

Never mind, father dear.   You have made a European reputation, and it's an exceedingly useful property, to me.   I like being the daughter of an eminent philologist, and one doesn't want religion to know one has got to be a good girl.

GERVAISE MASKELYNE, helplessly.

I left it all to your mother.

MODERNA.

Poor dear mother ! she used to tell us pretty little stories about Balaam and his ass, and the prophet Jonah.   I liked Grimm's *Tales* so much best.   I say, what did you make me look out Lawrence for ?

GERVAISE MASKELYNE.

Ah, you remind me. . . . There's a young fellow called Lawrence, it appears. .

MODERNA.

I know there is.   He's always about.

GERVAISE MASKELYNE, portentously.

Do you object to him ?

MODERNA, scenting a proposal.

I'm not particularly attached to him.

GERVAISE MASKELYNE.

What do you think of him ?

MODERNA.

I never do think of him.   I suffer him, that's all.

GERVAISE MASKELYNE.

Do you mind telling me your objection to him ?

MODERNA.

None whatever, there's nothing to object to.   All men
are alike—all marriageable young men, I mean.   They
bore me.

GERVAISE MASKELYNE, feebly.

You must not talk like that.   Marriage was ordained—

MODERNA.

Oh, father, please don't *you* begin to talk like that, or I
shall have to go away.   It's no good.   It's so idiotic of
them to go and speak to you and spring these scenes on
me, when I could settle it all in a moment if they would
only tell *me* straight !

GERVAISE MASKELYNE.

I don't think you could . . . in this case . . . but I am confused. . . . Do I understand that you have a rooted objection to marriage as an institution, or is it only a personal dislike to this particular young man ?

MODERNA, sturdily.

Rooted objection to marriage as an institution.

GERVAISE MASKELYNE.

On what do you base these very strong convictions of yours, concerning the unadvisability of the step, may I ask ?

MODERNA.

Oh, I gave it a fair trial. I've been engaged once.
(Shivers.)

GERVAISE MASKELYNE.

And he jilted you ?

MODERNA.

I beg your pardon, father. I jilted him.

GERVAISE MASKELYNE.

Yes, yes, I remember now. A very worthy young man, if I mistake not ? . . .

MODERNA.

Very worthy, *too* worthy, "not low enough for me," as Queen Mary says.

GERVAISE MASKELYNE.

Not "low enough"! What is it you want ? You seem to have some most extraordinary notions. I hope you are not intending to present me with a Villon for a son-in-law, for I tell you frankly, I will not receive any one' without at least four quarterings. But now about this young Lawrence?

MODERNA.

Oh, father, haven't I said enough? Please let us say no more about it. He's very nice, and good, and proper, and dull, and all that; but I don't care for him, and I simply can't marry him.

GERVAISE MASKELYNE, searching among his papers.

But my dear child, . . . you mistake. . . . Where is that note I made? It is not you he wants, . . . it's Verona . . . at least I think so. (Searching frantically.)

MODERNA, shrieking with laughter.

Verona! Oh, father, did you really make a note of it?

GERVAISE MASKELYNE, nervously.

I may have done so . . . your mother came in when I was very busy and told me something of a young man who wanted to marry my daughter . . . Verona, . . . it appears . . . yes, here is the paper!

MODERNA, aside.

And I thought, like the conceited idiot I am, it was me. Verona—of course it's Verona! I remember now . . . at Merrow. . . .

GERVAISE MASKELYNE.

And I was minded to ask you, being the eldest, and possessed, I believe, of a fair modicum of ordinary intelligence, what you thought of the young man. He is well off, I hear, which is an important consideration to an impecunious man - of - letters. Still, as your opinion is distinctly unfavourable, I shall signify as much to your mother; and then I hope I shall be left in peace.

MODERNA, wildly.

Stop—stop—father! He's a dear—he's perfectly sweet —he's charming! . . .

GERVAISE MASKELYNE.

Eh, what? You've changed your mind?

MODERNA.

Not *my* mind—Verona's mind. He's the very person to suit her, and he adores her, and she likes him I fancy . . . I think . . . in fact I'm sure she does. Oh, father, say he may; you have nothing against him, have you?

GERVAISE MASKELYNE, drily.

Nothing but the unfavourable opinion of my eldest daughter.

MODERNA.

I only meant he wouldn't suit *me*—or I him. You see I'm so scatter-brained, and so reckless, and erratic, and tiresome, I should make any ordinary man perfectly miserable.

GERVAISE MASKELYNE, sneering.

You mean that it would take something extremely superior and extraordinary in the way of a man to attract you?

MODERNA, humbly.

Only an extraordinary man would put up with *me*; I'm not nice or reasonable. I couldn't be happy with a thoroughly nice, good, clever man. It would take a mixture of god and devil that does not exist to bear with me, and make *me* happy—and even then I shouldn't make *him* happy; so you see (smiling) I have very wisely decided to remain a bachelor girl.

GERVAISE MASKELYNE.

A bachelor girl! I don't recognise the expression. . . . Tchlk! Tchlk! You have completely wasted my morning—you and Verona between you!

MODERNA.

I'll go . . . Only, father, please be nice to Tom.

GERVAISE MASKELYNE.

Is he Tom already? Well, I'll be as nice as I can. . . . Will it be necessary for me to ascertain Verona's sentiments on the subject?

MODERNA, laughing.

Oh no! Not the least need. Leave Verona to me. I'll look after her. (Going.)

GERVAISE MASKELYNE.

It is you, madam, I think, who need looking after. I intend to devote to you some of my best attention— when I have shown up my friend the Professor's absurdities in the *Journal of Philology*.

MODERNA.

Ah, do !   Till then, I must get along as well as I can !
(Blows him a kiss and departs.)

XVIII.

Mr. and Mrs. GERVAISE MASKELYNE
request the pleasure of the company of

----

at the marriage of their daughter,
VERONA ALICE,
with Mr. THOMAS BOURCHIER LAWRENCE,
at St. Paul's, Knightsbridge,
at 2.30 o'clock,
and afterwards, at 280 Queen's Gate.

R.S.V.P.

IN THE LIBRARY, 10 A.M.

PEGGY, dictatorially.

Now look here, William ; you won't " rag," will you—
not even Aunt Eliza ?

WILLIAM, earnestly.

No, 'pon honour, I won't.   I'll be as grave as a judge
on the bench, or—

PEGGY.

An Eton boy in chapel will do.   And oh, I say, see
that Tom has the soles of his boots darkened.   If I see
two large white ghosts sticking up in front of me during
the ceremony I shall laugh, I know I shall.

L

WILLIAM.

What a horrid girl you are, Peggy. You laugh just like a hyæna! Very well, if you will leave it to me, I'll manage Tom.

PEGGY.

And, William, I rely on you to look after Aunt Eliza, and keep her quiet. Now don't say silly things, and make her giggle—at *her* age—and swallow crumbs the wrong way. The honour of the family is in your hands. But you mustn't offend her. You must suppress her without letting her know she's suppressed; and if she does make herself ridiculous, you must contrive to let everybody know she's fearfully rich.

WILLIAM.

I'll introduce her to Billy Danvers. It will be awfully good sport. I bet you, he'll chaff her to death, and she'll never even guess he's making fun of her.

PEGGY.

No, that won't do at all. You must keep her in the background, and entertain her. Immolate yourself!

WILLIAM.

What a fearful snob you are to want to hide her! Every family has got an Aunt Eliza they would like to keep dark, and that's bound to show at these sort of gatherings. Make the best of her, I say. Look at the Lawrences' comic uncle, just returned from what he calls Cape o' D'ope! He and Aunt Eliza could buy us all up, I suppose.

PEGGY.

Well, introduce them to each other.   I leave it to you.

Exit.

WILLIAM.

You've got to leave something to somebody.   You can't manage everything yourself.   By Jove, now, if Peggy was a fellow, wouldn't one just lick her !

*   *   *   *   *

In Verona's Room, 1 p.m.

PEGGY, tendering a plate of rice pudding to VERONA.

Here, you must eat something, or you'll faint.   What possessed you to burst out crying at lunch ?

VERONA.

It was—the last lunch !—(Cries anew.)

PEGGY.

What rubbish !   One would think you were going to die, instead of only getting married.   Here, eat, do, or I shall have you fainting on my hands.   (A knock at the door.) *Who* is it ?

SERVANT.

Mr. Lawrence, miss, wants to know if he can speak to Miss Verona for one minute ?

PEGGY.

No, of *course* he can't ; how dare the bridegroom come to the bride's house on the day of the wedding?   He ought to know better.

MODERNA, coming in.

Peggy, what a martinet you are! Go and speak to Tom. Perhaps he has something particular to say? I will go on feeding Verona.

PEGGY.

Perhaps he has lost the licence. He's idiot enough for anything.

Exit.

VERONA, faintly.

Peggy rather takes one's breath away; she is so *very* managing. And I should have liked to see Tom. (Wistfully.)

MODERNA.

You'll see him in half an hour, dear. Do eat, for Tom's sake!

VERONA, heroically swallowing a spoonful of rice.

Yes, I will. Isn't he sweet, Moderna?

MODERNA.

Yes, dear. Delightful. Another?

VERONA, imbibes another spoonful.

Aren't I good? Dear Tom! Oh, I wish there was another of him for you, dear.

MODERNA.

Not *quite* the same, or you would be jealous.

VERONA.

Oh no, I shouldn't. I should so like you to be happy too. He's so gentle and yet manly, don't you think so?

MODERNA.

Yes, dear, he really is.

VERONA.

And don't you think him awfully good-looking?

MODERNA.

Oh, awfully.

VERONA.

And the noble way he has of throwing back his head, and looking at you! . . . Moderna!

MODERNA.

What, dear?

VERONA.

I don't really think you like Tom.

MODERNA.

What an idea! Why not?

VERONA.

Because you are so grudging in your praise.

MODERNA.

My *dear* Verona! I think he's charming. Did I not say so? Now, shall I tell you something?

VERONA.

Yes.

MODERNA.

I don't think you'll be *quite* happy, unless I own that I
am a little bit jealous of you.

VERONA, pensively.

I suppose not; but then he is so very sweet, isn't he?
He—

MODERNA, impatiently.

We ought to stick on your veil now. . . . These real orange
flowers will give you an awful headache, I'm afraid?. . .

VERONA.

Oh, I don't mind. Put them on. I like them to be
real, and come all the way from Nice.

MODERNA.

By way of Paris ! . . .   Stand still. . . .

IN THE HALL, 2 P.M.

MRS. MASKELYNE, suspiciously, meeting her husband.

Ahem ! where are you going, Gervaise?

GERVAISE MASKELYNE.

My dear . . . to my club as usual . . . I believe.

MRS. MASKELYNE.

Please to remember that you have to give your daughter
away at half-past two, and it is now ten minutes past.

GERVAISE MASKELYNE.

True, my dear . . . I was forgetting. You should have given me a written note. I will come back at once.

MRS. MASKELYNE.

But you can't give her away in that coat.

GERVAISE MASKELYNE.

True, my dear, but what am I to do?

MRS. MASKELYNE.

Change it, of course. There, quick, you have only five minutes. (Bundles him into his dressing-room.)

GERVAISE MASKELYNE.

I am as wax in your hands. (Aside.) In another moment I should have been off comfortably to the Club. . . .

MRS. MASKELYNE.

And I'm not ready myself. (Calls gently.) Aurélie! Minching!

MINCHING, in the corridor.

There! The old lady's a-yelling for you, Miss Aurelia.

AURÉLIE.

I go! I go! Miss Peggy she just dance on her hat, and I mend it. It not becoming, she say.

*   *   *   *   *

IN THE SIDE AISLE, 2.30 P.M.

THOMSON OF BRASENOSE.

I say, I think old Tom's got the best of the bunch, don't
you ?   A nice, quiet, modest, little thing !

GRAHAM OF TRINITY.

With no eyes for anybody or anything but Tom, eh ?
Good form, you know, even if it's not genuine.   She's
doing the part all right.

THOMSON OF BRASENOSE.

How do you like the little sister, Peggy, with her eyes
all over the place ?

GRAHAM OF TRINITY.

Only a puppy—too much tongue !   Wants a month's
cubbing, and a steady whip.

THOMSON OF BRASENOSE.

How about the eldest ?

GRAHAM OF TRINITY.

Nice girl enough—rather flighty, but runs pretty straight
as yet.   'See later on in the season.

THOMSON OF BRASENOSE.

Well, I don't know.   She's a deuced deal too morbid
for me.   Writes poetry, I'm told.   " Come and kiss me
when I'm dead " kind of thing.   Shouldn't have time
for a girl like that, thank you !

GRAHAM OF TRINITY.

That's only her rot.   She doesn't know what she's talking about half the time.   I believe, if you really knew
her, that girl is just about as good and simple as they
make 'em.

THOMSON OF BRASENOSE.

Not my style, at any rate.   I prefer something like the
other bridesmaid, Miss Fleming—isn't that her name?
Give me a girl who, etc.

*   *   *   *   *

IN THE MORNING-ROOM, 3 O'CLOCK

ARTHUR DEVEREL, in a whisper to his sister-in-law, who has
driven him back from church.

Do oblige me by rubbing off some of that powder.   It's
too awfully obvious.

MRS. FRED DEVEREL, *née* FLOSSIE RENSSELAER, gingerly
applying a handkerchief.

There, is that better?

ARTHUR DEVEREL.

More, more !   You take good care not to affect it.

MRS. FRED DEVEREL, plaintively.

I *really* am not *sure* I put any on at all.

ARTHUR DEVEREL, sneering.

Your maid did then.   You must rub it off.   I can't
have my sister-in-law look like a second-rate actress.

MRS. FRED DEVEREL, significantly.

Talk about actresses !   Look at that girl you jilted !

ARTHUR DEVEREL.

Miss Maskelyne?   I beg your pardon, Flossie, everybody knows she jilted me.

MRS. FRED DEVEREL.

Every one knows you say so—it's part of your ridiculous
code; but I know better, and I'm truly glad she didn't
come into the family.   Just look what a colour she's
got !

ARTHUR DEVEREL.

Do you mean to insinuate that Miss Maskelyne is
made-up ?

MRS. FRED DEVEREL.

If she hasn't rouged, she has been drinking *eau de Cologne*,
at any rate.   Look at her cheeks !

ARTHUR DEVEREL, sententiously.

Excitement.

MRS. FRED DEVEREL.

You mean because she is talking to Lord Coniston ?
Yes, most girls flush when he speaks to them.   I fancy
they would all like to get him if they could.

ARTHUR DEVEREL, stiffly.

Are you not aware that he proposed to Moderna ?

MRS. FRED DEVEREL, excitedly.

Prop... what?... did he really? I remember something
about it. Well, he won't give her the chance again in a
hurry. He's disgusted with her. Everybody is.

ARTHUR DEVEREL.

Because she gets prettier every day?

MRS. FRED DEVEREL, very angry.

Because she gets queerer every day. Goodness knows
I'm not straight-laced, but the things that girl does!
Did you hear of her going out as lady's maid to old
Lady Kernaway, to see what it was like? And then
writing about it in a daily paper afterwards? And selling
in a shop all day in a village in Surrey? Fancy poor
old Coniston married to a woman like that!

ARTHUR DEVEREL, severely.

I must say, Flossie, I think these remarks of yours are
in rather questionable taste, considering that you are her
mother's guest, and that I heard you a moment ago
begging and praying her to make one of your house-
party in the autumn.

MRS. FRED DEVEREL.

Oh, that's nothing. These sort of girls are enormously
in request. They make a thing go. I shall make a
point of having her at Bleahope. I shall ask little
Violet Fleming as a foil. You'll come, Arthur?

ARTHUR DEVEREL.

Well, I daresay I shall look you up at Bleahope—sometime.   (She smiles malignly.)

IN THE DINING-ROOM, 4 O'CLOCK

UNCLE TOM, of the LAWRENCES.

A glass of champagne, Miss Maskelyne?

AUNT ELIZA, of the MASKELYNES.

A weeny, teeny, little sip.   Just to taste.

UNCLE TOM.

Nonsense about sips; you must drink the bride's health
properly.   Here's to Verona Lawrence; and stop—
while I am about it—here's to the health of the chief
bridesmaid; she's the one for my money.

AUNT ELIZA.

Ay, she's the best of them, though she is no the bonniest.

UNCLE TOM.

I say she's the prettiest—and the cleverest.   Knows
how to sling a barrel, by Jove!

AUNT ELIZA.

"Sling a barrel," Mr. Lawrence?. What will that be?

UNCLE TOM.

I'll tell you how it began.   She was bragging a bit at
dinner last night, as girls will, you know, and I asked

her, just to stump her, if she knew how to sling a barrel
—and blest, if she didn't take an orange and a ribbon
off her fan and sling it as if she had been a drayman.
That's the girl for me.   I'd have chosen her for Tom if
he'd consulted me.   Well, well, her turn next, I suppose.
I'm sorry I've no more nephews.   Who's that boy she's
talking to now?   Do you know?

AUNT ELIZA.

Troth, and I do.   Danvers, or something like that.   A
bonny lad, but a freevolous.   I declare after I had been
talking to him for a quarter of an hour, I didn't know if
I was standing on my head or my heels.   Such jokes
as he was putting on me—

UNCLE TOM.

Boys will be boys, you are aware.

AUNT ELIZA.

Ay, if they would; it's when they will be old men, that
it beats me.

*   *   *   *   *

IN THE DRAWING-ROOM, 4.30 O'CLOCK

LADY RIDDELL, to MODERNA.

Well, young woman, how are you?   So you have lived
to dance at your sister's wedding in green slippers, eh?

MODERNA.

Thank you, dear aunt, I'm bearing up wonderfully.
Don't trouble to condole with me.   (Laughing.)

LADY RIDDELL.

Condolence? Rubbish! I condole with a girl for not getting married! No. You must go in for being useful. We want workers. I must see if I cannot get you on to some of our Committees.

MODERNA, laughing.

But I have no opinions at all, Aunt.

LADY RIDDELL.

No more had Cecilia, at your age. At any rate you can work; and the opinions will come in time! I'll write to you. By the way, I shouldn't be so intimate with that dimpled devil yonder, if I were you.

MODERNA.

Dimpled devil! Billy Danvers! Oh, Aunt, he's a dear. I've known him ages. He's my "play boy," as the Americans say.

LADY RIDDELL.

I don't advise you to play with him too much. It's an ungrateful mean face. Well, no matter. See for yourself. By the bye, Cecilia sent her love! She's a regular backslider, if you like. No good at all. Jekyll and Jekyll's babies! . . .

MODERNA.

She's happy, at any rate.

LADY RIDDELL.

A mere lotus-eater! 'Give her up. 'Adopt you, if you like. Think of it. Good-bye.

Exit.

IN THE CONSERVATORY, 5 O'CLOCK

BILLY DANVERS.

Oh, here you are ! I've been looking for you. You're
as pale as a ghost. Sit down. Well, how did the bride
go off? Did she weep?

MODERNA.

She did the usual thing.

BILLY DANVERS.

You wept during the service—I saw you.

MODERNA, affectionately.

You lie, Billy.

BILLY DANVERS.

Well, it impressed Coniston very much. Do you know,
Mod, I can't help thinking that he's got a sneaking
kindness for *you*.

MODERNA, scornfully.

Do you really, Billy?

BILLY DANVERS.

Yes ; and I am sure—and I have an eye for these things
—you could bring him to the point in a minute, if you
chose? Do—do, and ask me down to Coniston for the
shooting. Isn't that an inducement?

MODERNA.

The greatest?

BILLY DANVERS.

And I'll give you *such* a wedding present.   I'm awfully good at wedding presents.

MODERNA.

Can't do it, dear boy.

BILLY DANVERS.

Why ?   Do you consider Coniston such a confirmed Benedict as all that ?

MODERNA.

How do you know that it isn't me that's a confirmed . . . ?

BILLY DANVERS.

—Benedicta !   Ah, but you've *been addicted* to it so long, no one believes in you.

MODERNA.

Oh, Billy, what an awful pun !

BILLY DANVERS.

It was your aunt who corrupted me !   We got on beautifully, do you know ?   I make a point of getting on with old ladies, as a provision for my old age.   She actually asked me to take her to "one of those new Opera Buffaloes !"   Wouldn't Letty Lind give her fits ?

MODERNA.

Billy, I do not permit you to laugh at my relations.
(Yawns.)   I'm too tired to talk.   (Pettishly.)   Do go.

BILLY DANVERS.

Here comes Coniston. (Aside.) I'll slope.

CONISTON.

I'm so glad you've got rid of that dreadful *fin de siècle* boy. Sit down a minute. It has gone off very well, hasn't it? And your father managed to give away the right daughter after all, and your mother didn't sob too audibly, and William showed us how young Eton can behave, and Peggy wasn't too fussy, and you—

MODERNA.

What was I?

CONISTON.

The prettiest bridesmaid I ever saw. But now both you and your bouquet look tired. Well, good-bye. I'm off by the Club train to-night.

MODERNA.

Where are you going?

CONISTON.

To Paris—Milan eventually. I thought of attending the celebration of the rite of St. Ambrose there. Then Constantinople. Then . . . I have let Coniston, and my old barrack in Grosvenor Square, for two years, you know. . . . I don't suppose I shall be settled in town before that time—

MODERNA.

You are nearly as restless as I am,

M

CONISTON.

I like to see everything.

MODERNA.

So do I . . . and I mean to . . . in my limited way. When you come back we will tell each other of our discoveries. We shall hear from you, I suppose?

CONISTON, sadly.

Peggy has promised to correspond with me. . . . Good-bye.   Exit.

IN THE HALL, 6 O'CLOCK.

GERVAISE MASKELYNE.

Why, my dear Verona . . . still here? I thought I had said good-bye to you an hour ago? Where's Tom?

MODERNA.

It's me—Moderna, father.

GERVAISE MASKELYNE, writhing.

A—ie! Couldn't "me—Moderna" use better grammar?

MODERNA.

Too tired, father.

GERVAISE MASKELYNE.

So am I. These weddings—ah, well—they are a little exhausting! Allow a decent interval to elapse before you ask me to give *you* away, that's a good girl.

MODERNA, with decision.

I'll *never* ask you at all!

XIX

EXTRACTS FROM LETTERS, ETC.

From MODERNA'S Diary.

June 9th.—The last entry in this diary was on the day of Verona's wedding, nearly two years ago—and it strikes me as terribly naïve ? That was the old me. It frightens me to see how different the new me is. But I won't burn it, I will only write Finis, and keep it as a human document. . . .

From PEGGY MASKELYNE, Queen's Gate, London, to Lord CONISTON, Rome.

. . . Some of those Roman *fazzoletti*, you know, to make a dress of. Moderna's love ; she's too busy to write. . . .

From Mrs. FRED DEVEREL to her brother-in-law, ARTHUR DEVEREL.

. . . find out which of the Maskelyne girls Coniston *did* propose to four years ago? I know it was one of them. He was secretary to old Maskelyne before he came into the title, and almost lived in the house, and saw the girls every day. It can't have been that little cat Peggy, and Verona is too sensible for anything . . .

From ARTHUR DEVEREL to Mrs. FRED DEVEREL.

. . . Absolutely decline to make any inquiries regarding the subject you mention. It concerns neither of us. . . .

. . . Father is ordered abroad for the winter. They are going to let the house. Moderna declares she won't go with them. She wants to go and live in a flat with a *dreadful* girl, a Miss Tremaine, a journalist. . . .

. . . Don't forget,—dinner at eight. I want you to take down a Mr. Brown. He's an East End clergyman, and a cousin of my husband's, and rather dull. I know, though, you can make him talk. He will fall a victim at once, but he would be no good to you, I'm afraid. But at any rate, don't, dear, I beg of you, flaunt your hansoms and your latch-keys and all the rest of it in his face, or talk about music halls or French novels. *I* know you haven't, but he is sure to fancy you have read the one and been to the other, if you talk of them. . . .

. . . the experiments of a young lady in society, as a lady's maid in one of the best families, lately given to the world in the columns of the *Incontrovertible*. It is no secret that this audacious young pioneer is a daughter of one of our most prominent professors, a man of well-known repute in social, literary, and scientific circles. . . .

From the " Incontrovertible."

Why are all young poets so consistently, so irretrievably melancholy? Here we have a little poem, by M. E. Maskelyne, of very fair average merit, but, which for settled gloom and concentrated despair beats anything we have seen for a long time. Only extreme youth on the part of the authoress could justify such "mortuary reflections," as Mark Twain would call them. . . .

From DOLLY TREMAINE, 500B Strand, to Miss MASKELYNE.

. . . You won't fail me, old girl, will you? for it is not everybody I would ask. I must have a girl, don't you know, with some go, and no nonsense about her, or else she spoils the whole thing. Bring your . . .

BILLY DANVERS to MODERNA.

. . . there's a dear. I am in a devil of a hole . . . do arrange to say a good word for me to father . . . You can do anything with him, and this is one of *my worst.* . . .   .

CECILIA JEKYLL to VERONA LAWRENCE.

. . . I haven't heard about this Miss Tremaine. Moderna never writes to me now. She has got into a very bad set, I hear. Francis says she is out and out a good sort, and that there never was a straighter girl—that she will get over this phase—and "it will all come out in the wash"—isn't my husband slangy? . . .

Lady RIDDELL to her daughter CECILIA JEKYLL.

. . . Moderna is all right.   Let her alone.   Every girl ought to have a Wanderjahr.   So would you, if you hadn't married. . . .

XX

IN a conservatory opening out of a ball-room.   Captain HEAVISIDE, R.N., is sitting with Mrs. MORTIMER.   As the music strikes up he rises.

CAPTAIN HEAVISIDE.

My dance with Miss Maskelyne—oh, by Jove, I must not miss that !

MRS. MORTIMER, sarcastically.

Oh, by Jove, no.   Good-bye for the present.   (Enter Darcy.)   Well, Jack, your face looks crumpled.   You've been thinking.

DARCY.

Yes, very seriously.

MRS. MORTIMER.

At a dance !   Fie.

DARCY.

Oh, don't chaff.   I want you to help me.

MRS. MORTIMER.

I'll do anything for you—except dance with you.

DARCY, shortly.

I don't want you to dance with me.

MRS. MORTIMER.

Thank you.

DARCY.

At least not now.   But why do you say you won't?

MRS. MORTIMER.

Because I don't want my feet trod on every minute because you are watching Miss Maskelyne instead of minding your steps—she *does* mind her steps very prettily, and I suspect her of private skirt dancing—to be your partner in the Lancers so that you may be Miss Maskelyne's *vis-a-vis ;* to be brought up sharp in a waltz so that you may stop where Miss Maskelyne is fanning herself and talking to her partner—

DARCY.

Heavens !   Do you mean to say that you notice all that?

MRS. MORTIMER.

The state of your affections is patent to the meanest eye, Jack.   And Moderna is rather a friend of mine.   I've known her ever since she came out, you know.

DARCY, eagerly.

Yes, I know—

MRS. MORTIMER.

—But I think she should not be allowed to devastate a ball-room in this way.   She's a very pretty girl and not a bit *passée*, but it is time she selected a victim—a permanent victim, I say, and cleared the decks for Peggy. The poor girl hasn't a chance when her sister's present.

DARCY.

I can't stand Peggy. I always think of that quotation— "an idiot full of sound and fury, signifying nothing"!

MRS. MORTIMER.

She chaffs you, I suppose, or daren't she? I wonder you don't fall in love with her? She is your own age, while her sister Moderna is a year older than you.

DARCY.

What's that got to do with it?

MRS. MORTIMER.

In every possible way she is older. My poor boy, she wouldn't suit you a bit. She could gallop all round you in five minutes.

DARCY.

Oh, I know she's sharp and all that, but after all, a man is master in the end—if only he knows how to exert his authority properly.

MRS. MORTIMER.

If only! And do you think you are the man to—we will say "influence" a headstrong girl like that? Remember she has had her way ever since she came out,

that her father's a savant, and her mother's a fool, and
that neither have ever been able to control her in the
least.   I am the only person who has any influence over
her, and she thinks me almost too respectable and old
fashioned.   She tells me of all her escapades though.
She has done everything—tried everything—got bored
over everything—don't you think she would get bored
with you, sooner or later?

DARCY.

Everything happens—sooner or later.   I'm not a fool.
I know she is a modern woman and all that—has gone
in for being independent, don't you know, and trying
everything—and all that sort of thing.   I don't care.
One ought to let a woman have a try at things, just
to let her see what a mess she makes of it!—and, hang
it all, a girl must marry in the end, you know!

MRS. MORTIMER.

Oh, must she?   Well, I daresay you are right.   She
may be getting tired of it.   She's had plenty of fun.
You might try?   .

DARCY.

The worst of it is, she is so confoundedly enigmatical.
Most girls make up their minds long before a fellow
does, and can't help letting him see it, but Miss Maskelyne's always so awfully polite. . . .

MRS. MORTIMER.

You mean she won't flirt with you?

DARCY, shuddering.'

Oh no! I have never even made love to her. But still she might drop the mask sometimes.

MRS. MORTIMER.

In your favour? Well, ask her like a man.

DARCY.

And risk a refusal?

MRS. MORTIMER, sarcastically.

The chances against you are infinitesimal! And as good men as you have risked the contingency.

DARCY, pulling up his collar.

I have never given myself away yet, and I don't mean to. But I wish I were not so abominably *épris*.

MRS. MORTIMER.

It's awkward, certainly. Those are the accents of truth ! I am sorry for you, but what can I do for you?

DARCY.

A good deal. You can find out for me—

MRS. MORTIMER.

"Which way her affections tend?" Ask Peggy?

DARCY.

Heaven forbid!

MRS. MORTIMER.

Peggy knows, of course. Sisters always do.

DARCY.

Well, I shan't ask that minx. It's *you* I want to help me. You can. I only want you to watch her. They're all here, confound them !

MRS. MORTIMER.

Who ?

DARCY.

My possible rivals. I mean this evening to be decisive. She is going up to Scotland to her sister's on Thursday, and they have asked me too, and I should like it settled before—make the visit so much pleasanter. Let me see ? (Counts on his fingers.) There is Bingham, and that ass Heaviside, and Deverel, that old flame of hers—

MRS. MORTIMER.

The man she jilted ?

DARCY.

Deserved it, pompous ass ! However, he wants to have it on again, so I must count him.

MRS. MORTIMER.

Is that all ?

DARCY.

That's really all. There's a parson called Brown who hangs about, but he's absolutely out of it. Those are the only three I'm at all afraid of, and I'm not really afraid of them. There's Bingham, her mother likes Bingham, thinks he will be civil to her when she's his mother-in-law. Good for Bingham, but he won't get the girl—she laughs at him. Then Deverel—I don't think Deverel has any chance. He muffed it so before.

MRS. MORTIMER.

How about Heaviside?

DARCY.

Oh, we needn't bother about him. She takes him in to supper. I fancy she's nursing him for Peggy.

MRS. MORTIMER.

Well, Jack, I think I see. You wish me to read, mark, and inwardly digest the significance of the glances she bestows on the three gentlemen you have named.

DARCY.

Glances! Oh, heavens!

MRS. MORTIMER.

Jealous already? Now go away and leave me to conduct my observations in peace—it has to happen to-night, you say. Go. Don't you see (laughing) you prevent people who are not in love with Miss Maskelyne, coming to ask me to dance?

Exit DARCY.

LATER ON.   IN THE BALL-ROOM.

DARCY, eagerly to Mrs. MORTIMER.

Well?

MRS. MORTIMER.

I've found out nothing as yet, except that she looks bored to death.   She hasn't got what she wants, I can tell you that much.

DARCY.

Ah—our dance hasn't come off yet. . . .

MRS. MORTIMER.

Is she as easily pleased as that?   Do go away, you un-settle me.   I shall know all by the end of the evening. Meet me at the foot of the stairs in an hour's time.

LATER STILL.   AT THE DOOR OF THE BALL-ROOM.

MODERNA, to BINGHAM.

Oh, Mr. Bingham, I am so very sorry to have to cut our dance, but I am going.   I am so tired.   Don't I look it?

BINGHAM, enthusiastically.

On the contrary, you look—   (She passes on.)

  *   *   *   *   *

HEAVISIDE, meeting her.

Oh Miss Maskelyne, this is too bad of you—you promised I should take you in to supper !

MODERNA.

I must ask you to let me break my promise. I am so dreadfully tired. I should eat nothing, and that would bore you—good-night ! (She passes on.)

    *   *   *   *   *

DEVEREL, meeting her.

May I come and call to-morrow, Miss Maskelyne ?

MODERNA, effusively.

Yes, do, Mr. Deverel. Heaps of people are coming. Peggy and I go to Scotland on Thursday.

DEVEREL.

Why do you always ask me to see you in a crowd ?

MODERNA, smiling.

It's the way I like to see you best. (Aside.) Never another tête-à-tête with him as long as I live. (Aloud.) Don't forget ! (Passes on.)

    *   *   *   *   *

ON THE STAIRS.

CONISTON, languidly.

Have you got a dance for me, Moderna ? I've just come.

MODERNA, brusquely.

And I'm just going . . . good-bye. (Passes on.)

*   *   *   *   *

DARCY, who has followed with PEGGY, to Mrs. MORTIMER at the
foot of the stairs.

Well ?.

MRS. MORTIMER.

Well ?   You have completely spoilt my evening for me !

DARCY.

I am so eternally obliged to you.   Well—?   It's all
right, isn't it ?

MRS. MORTIMER, smiling malignly.

You needn't be afraid of Bingham. . . .

DARCY, fervently.

Thank heaven !

MRS. MORTIMER.

Nor of Heaviside !   Nor of Deverel !

DARCY.

Thank heaven again !   Now I breathe freely.   I shall
call there to-morrow.

MRS. MORTIMER.

Better not.

DARCY.

Why not ?   I rely implicitly on your judgment.   I shall
ask Miss—

MRS. MORTIMER.

Are you really quite blind and deaf, Jack Darcy?

DARCY.

What do you mean? I noticed nothing. Please tell me, quick.

MRS. MORTIMER.

I'll just tell you one thing. If that girl ever marries, it will be the man she spoke to on the stairs just now. Help me with my cloak. I'll drive you home.

*   *   *   *   *

DARCY, dropping the window of the brougham.

Are you really sure? Coniston? Why, she has known him ages—ever since she came out. . . .

MRS. MORTIMER.

What of that?

DARCY.

I believe he proposed to her once, and she refused him. At least I heard some fellows say so at the Club.

MRS. MORTIMER.

She was only a baby, and didn't know her own mind then.

DARCY.

And do you mean that he has hung about her ever since hoping to make her change it?

MRS. MORTIMER.

He's not such a fool. I don't suppose he has ever said another word about it to her. He goes about and lives his life. But I'm perfectly certain that he never meant or means to marry any other woman. Put it like that if you like. He isn't one of your whiners, but he knows what he wants.

DARCY.

And do you think she cares for him?

MRS. MORTIMER.

Didn't you see her eyes? didn't you hear her voice? She cares for him, but without knowing it. He has gone the right way with her. That sort of girl always ends by marrying the man who has the strength of mind to wait for her.

DARCY.

Well, I can't say Coniston looks at all like a love-sick swain. And he's just going to sail that yacht of his to America. Why doesn't he stay in town and make love to her.

MRS. MORTIMER.

Pas si bête ! That would not be the way to fetch Moderna.

DARCY.

And he has had all sorts of affairs since ! They say he is engaged to that Frenchwoman . . . Madame Belin-fante. . . .

MRS. MORTIMER.

I don't believe a word of it.

N

DARCY.

Then there was that flirtation with Lady—

MRS. MORTIMER, curtly.

I suppose you will agree that he is a man of the world?

DARCY.

Oh yes, of course,—goes everywhere—has everything right—very much in it—

MRS. MORTIMER.

Very well, then!

XXI

Tom Lawrence's shooting in Perthshire. Verona Lawrence and Moderna are sitting waiting for the guns.

VERONA.

The men will be here soon. I see their smoke over there. I'm hungry, are not you?

MODERNA.

I am never hungry now.

VERONA.

You go out too much. How many nights were you out last week?

MODERNA.

Every night, I think—but I forget.   It's an awful bore, going out.   (Sighing.)

VERONA, sharply.

Why do you do it then?

MODERNA.

Please, Verona, don't pretend to be unsophisticated. Two years of marriage can't have done all that.   Why do I go out?   Because I can't help it, I suppose.

VERONA, sturdily.

Why can't you help it?

MODERNA.

Because . . . I don't know . . . if one once leaves off . . . one doesn't want to drop out altogether . . . oh, don't be silly, Verona, you know it all as well as I do. . . .

VERONA, sententiously.

You society girls always talk as if you were indispensable! I fancy society would get on very well without you, if you could only think so.   It does without *me*!

MODERNA, aside.

Verona never was pretty!   (Aloud.)   But the awful thing is that *I* can't get on without society.   I can't bear to stay at home, somehow.   I seem as if I must stand the racket, and dress, and do my hair, and

go out and talk to people who don't care twopence
about me.

VERONA, firmly.

Nonsense ! You are a pretty, lively girl, and people are
only too glad to see you and Peggy at their parties.
You help to make things go.

MODERNA, bitterly.

Oh yes. We are part of the furniture of a ball, or reception.
We are ordered in like rout seats, or ice plates. It
would never do not to ask the Maskelynes ! But oh,
how tired I am of all the wretched, selfish, commonplace *routine* of going out . . . seeing the insides of
other people's houses, eating other people's suppers, night
after night. . . .

VERONA, drily.

You must be a pleasant sort of guest to have !

MODERNA.

My dear, you don't suppose I am so rude as to allow
my hostess to see I am bored. I am quite equal to
making her, and everybody else, think I am enjoying
myself when I am not, but oh, how cross I am when I
get home ! I just gulp down my beef-tea, and go up to
bed without a word. I never discuss partners with
Peggy. I do not remember them—or they me. Why
should they ? I know everybody and everybody knows
me. Nobody ever asks to be introduced now—they
all have been some time or other, if they could remember. . . .

VERONA, carelessly.

Well, you *have* been out a good time. . . . Look at that heron up there !

MODERNA.

I don't care for herons . . . I should like to go away for a little—like Ogier the Dane—and come back. . . . I could "come out" again, and be very shy, and wear a little tulle—y dress "trimmed daisies." (Makes a little mental excursion to her dressmaker.)

VERONA.

I don't think you *could* be shy—or dignified either— you are just yourself. But as for being young again— don't you think men are very glad to meet a nice girl who knows her way about, and can talk sensibly?

MODERNA.

Yes, I daresay, as a sort of solid background to fluffy giggling innocence, one is tolerated—but the most intelligent man in the world would leave one in a moment for a girl with red arms—and whose first ball it was !

VERONA.

My dear girl, you are not so old as all that—only twenty-four.

MODERNA.

I feel a hundred. I don't care for anything or any one, so why should any one care for me ! I am sure I bore people. I am always the same. I can't even do my hair a different way. Nothing excites me. The maddest waltz does not make me flush or my pulse go quicker. I'm there, that's all—and I always wish I wasn't.

VERONA.

Marry.

MODERNA, angrily.

You all say that. It's idiotic, and it puts an end to conversation. You know I am never going to.

VERONA.

I know you say so.

MODERNA.

When I say a thing I mean it.

VERONA.

You ˙say that too. Well, but, really, my dear girl, if society bores you, I would give it up. Take to art again ?

MODERNA.

Art ! I soon saw what a duffer I was at that !

VERONA, patronisingly.

Write. You write very pretty little verses sometimes.

MODERNA.

All girls can scribble a little. And I should never get my things into magazines if it weren't for Dolly Tremaine. What I want is some really absorbing interest in life.

VERONA.

Why don't you take an interest in my children? They are sadly in want of a good aunt.

MODERNA, sneering.

Be Aunt Moderna, and keep the family "log," and chronicle the growth and movements of the family—and knit the socks—and take the invalids to the seaside— no, thank you!

VERONA, stolidly.

It's all very well, but my contention is this. Even butterflies like you must settle down some time. You can't expect to have always a man at your feet, unless you marry one.

MODERNA.

What, marry the poor creature in order to keep him there—bind him against his inclination! That is the most selfish policy I have ever heard!

VERONA.

It's every girl's policy. Once a woman has got to a certain age, she ought to have found one person who is sworn to think her perfect for the rest of her existence— the most beautiful woman in the world to him!

MODERNA.

To him! That is such an insulting addition!

VERONA.

Then find some one who thinks you beautiful to the rest of the world as well, and who will be jealous of you

and make your life a burden to you. What is amiss
with Mr. Brown ?

MODERNA.

Too earnest.

VERONA.

The earnest men make the best husbands. You are
far too flippant. And Mr. Donkin ?

MODERNA.

He offered to "make my life fuller and happier." The
very phrase offended me.

VERONA.

And Mr. Heaviside ? I asked him here for you.

MODERNA.

What waste ! He is impossible. No sense of humour.

VERONA.

And Coniston ? Why did you refuse him ? Be nice to
him when he comes back from America and bring it on
again ?

MODERNA.

He *is* back from America. He's in Paris now—and I
wouldn't for worlds bring it on again.

VERONA.

I don't suppose you could. Well, there's Mr. Darcy ?
He would marry you in a minute.

MODERNA.

Yes, if he could get *me* to propose! Too conceited. What's the good of talking about it? There's something wrong with every one. It is no good. I shall go back to town in a week, and it will all begin over again. I shall go out, and play the fool, and say spiteful things about other girls, and try to make people fall in love with me, and gossip, and talk scandal. . . . No, Verona, I shall give up society, with a large S, and go into Bohemia—there may be something new there, or I shall go on the stage—or take to type-writing—anything! I can't go on as I am doing now.

VERONA.

Take care—your eyes will be red! Oh, *please* don't! The men will be here directly—

MODERNA.

I don't care. . . . I don't care for anything . . . or anybody.

VERONA.

Really, Moderna, if I didn't know that you had no heart . . . I should think . . .

MODERNA.

What should you think?

VERONA, solemnly.

That you were in love. Are you?

MODERNA, violently.

In love! I wish I was! (A Pause.) Verona, are you shocked?

VERONA.

I hate to hear you talk like that.   Fancy *wanting* to be in love !

MODERNA, excitedly.

It would be something to live for, at any rate—something to get out of breath about, something to care for, to wait for, to be excited, to lie awake, to dream about ! Fancy the delicious moments of expectation,—the corresponding moods of despair !—the delight of opening letters eagerly, of hiding them—of making appointments, and keeping them,—of looking out of one's window at night, and wondering where, in all blue-grey London, he is at that moment—to be "in love"—to be . . .

VERONA.

You most extraordinary girl !   I should never have imagined. . . .   Well, then, if you feel like that, why not marry ? . . .

MODERNA, with a forced laugh.

I said I wanted to be in love ; I didn't say I wanted to be married.   That's quite a different thing.

VERONA, drawing herself up.

I think you are very rude—and very improper.

MODERNA.

Rude ?   My dear, I did not mean anything personal to *you !*

VERONA.

Then you mean I *don't* love my husband?

MODERNA, meditatively.

I don't know, I suppose you do.—Here come all the
men. Let's go and meet them!—but you "cheek"
him, you treat him like an old woman, more or less, you
say—I have often heard you—that you "know how to
manage him now." . . . Good heavens, talk of *managing*
the being you adore! . . . There's Mr. Heaviside and Tom.
Could I adore Mr. Heaviside, do you think, Verona
dear? I could manage him at any rate.

XXII

At the Academy Soirée.

MRS. MASKELYNE.

There they go! Peggy to supper with Billy Danvers, and
Moderna to look at her own portrait with Mr. Darcy!

I shall not see them again till the end of the evening.
It's not *de rigueur* now to come back to your chaperon,
Peggy tells me. It's not *de rigueur* to do anything one
does not want, I think.

If Peggy thinks Billy Danvers will ever propose to her,
she's mistaken. I could tell her—but she never
consults me. If he cares for anybody, it's Moderna, but
he is too selfish to care for anybody but himself.

No one will ever marry Peggy if she cultivates such a
sharp tongue. Every clever thing she says puts them

against her. Moderna's far cleverer, but there is a kind
of sweet silliness about her, that keeps her womanly.

They are my children after all, and I have the best
right to know all about them—and I do.

Yes, I could tell them things. I often know. Lookers-
on see most of the game. It's the fashion to treat a
mother as if she were blind, and saw nothing but
what she was told. But I see a great deal more than
they think. I often pretend I don't see things when I
do. It's less trouble. It's such hard work arguing with
girls. They turn everything round so, and even if one
isn't convinced, one has to say so for the sake of peace
and quietness. People ask me if I allow my daughters
to do this or that. " Allow ! " They do as they like.
It is the mothers who are not " allowed," who are sent
to school again—who are in a continual state of
tutelage, according to the present state of things. I am
continually putting my foot in it. I " don't understand."
I am not " up-to-date." Well, perhaps I don't want to
be ? Up-to-dateness seems to my benighted intellect
to mean bad manners, irresponsibility, flippancy, and to
speak plainly—selfishness.

I hate Ibsen. Moderna has seen lots of his plays.
She has got her life to live, she says. She must not
" repress her individuality," she must " develop her
personality." She wants to know, she wants to gain her
own experience, she doesn't care to make use of her
mother's before her. A mother is only a kind of helpless Survival of the Unfittest — to be trained and
educated and dragged up to date as far as her obtuse-
ness and obstinacy will allow.

I resent it, but I can't help it. I do my best to keep
pace with "modern thought." I read *Key-notes* and *The
Heavenly Twins*. It is as much as my place is worth to
look shocked at the terrible things people say in my own
drawing room, and, I am quite willing to wear fly-away
caps that don't fit, because they are fashionable.

Silly old stupid, matter-of-fact, practical Verona is my
only satisfactory daughter. She has married and settled
down, without any fuss and worry. She has got a nice
place in Scotland, and a house in town, and two pretty
children, and a husband who pets her, and takes care of
her—and yet, she was the plain one. . . .

Here comes Moderna. She has dropped Mr. Darcy,
and got a new escort, the man who put her into a
society novel the other day. *I* wouldn't speak to him,
but she doesn't seem to care. Poor Mr. Darcy cares
for her, I think. I wonder she doesn't shock him.
Poor child ! she looks sad, or is it her black dress which
is unbecoming ? She is getting very thin. She ought
to wear a necklace. People admire her for her "morbidezza" — I think they call it — people like Mr.
Tremaine, and want to paint her. Is it nice for a
mother to be told her daughter looks morbid ! And I
know it's only because she will do imprudent things and
take no care of her health. There never was a really
healthier girl than Moderna ; and she can be a rare
tomboy when she likes ! See her riding or playing
tennis, there is not much "morbidezza" about her
then !

No, thank you, Mr. Bingham, I'm quite comfortable
here. There is no draught, I assure you. No, I won't

have any refreshment, thank you.   I never do here,
there is such a struggle.

Why does he bother with an old woman like me?   I
hate being worried.   I want just to sit here and be let
alone, and close my eyes if I like.   They only worry
me by coming and offering me the brown-bread ice of
charity.   It's only cupboard civility at the best.   Mr.
Bingham is only polite to me because he's in love with
Moderna.

Lots of men are.   Nice men.   Men I should not
object to as sons - in - law.   Those are the men she
hates.   She prefers authors and actors, and people who
have "made their mark."   I like your clean, well-
shaven, fresh - complexioned young man, who doesn't
burn the midnight oil, and his eyes out over books, or
spoil his complexion with "make-up"; who isn't tragic,
or pedantic, or morbid—or anything except a gentleman.

There was Coniston.   I loved him as if he were my
own son.   He was so nice about the house.   I used to
consult him about things when he was Gervaise's secretary.   And I am sure he *once* cared for her.   He's
just come home, too.   Peggy had a letter.   She said he
was coming here to-night—but I don't see him.   I wish
Moderna could have cared for him.

I don't like my daughter's Bohemian friends.   There
are a lot of them here too to-night.   They may
have superlative genius — but they haven't ordinary
manners.   I don't like Mr. Kronofski, with the long
hair, and the grey complexion, and the bad teeth,
and the kind of smell of the foot-lights he brings with
him when he comes to call.   He's a musician, and

breaks the strings of my piano. I hate Miss Dolly
Tremaine—they call her D. T. in her own set—and
her slang, and her fast French stories, and her penny-a-
lining, and her cropped head. She sings Yvette Guil-
bert's songs with the improper verses that even Yvette
leaves out when she's over here. She lives in rooms
over an aerated bread-shop in the Strand, and calls
that "living in the odour of sanctity!" She's "Ceres"
in *Home-crops*, and "Sibyl" in the Wise Woman Series,
and takes presents from shops. She never seems to
have a regular meal, but she drinks brandies-and-sodas,
and reads the "Pink 'un." Moderna thinks her original,
and daring, and *fin de siecle*. I call her bad form, simply!

That's her brother Ned that Moderna is talking to
now. She is going to sit to him, I believe. I have no
particular objection to him, but it would be all the
same if I had. He's an impressionist—supposed to be
clever. I don't really understand what they mean by
impressionism. But it can't mean many sittings.

What time is it? Twelve! I hate this crowd and crush,
and for all the good I am I might as well be at home,
and in my bed. I yearn for my bed. But when I'm in
bed I can't sleep for listening for the sound of the latch-
key in the lock, so I may as well be here.

No, dearie, I'm not a bit tired. I don't think of going
home yet. I was only shutting my eyes because I was
thinking. I want a little talk with Mrs. Fleming, and I
have promised to go and look at your portrait with the
Admiral. Run away, dear, don't mind me. I'm all right.

Moderna's a good girl. It never occurs to Peggy to
come and see how I am getting on!

Who is she talking to? I declare I don't know. What a thing it is not to know one's own daughter's friends! She is making an appointment with the woman to go and dine. Where did she dine last night? I positively don't know. I suppose I was told.

They might be young men for all I know of their movements! They both have latch-keys, and they lose them continually, and the house is free to a certain number of burglars in consequence. It can't be helped. I oughtn't to be nervous, they say, and if I am, it's my own fault.

They generally do go out alone. I daresay it's best. Chaperons are not wanted under the present system. They chose to bring me to-night. I can't think why. "So nice of you to bring your mother, Miss Maskelyne," said Mrs. Rensselaer to Moderna as we came in. She sniggered, so I suppose it was meant for a joke, but I didn't like it—nor did Moderna, I could see.

What! Back again! My dear child, how pale you look! Want to go home? Are you bored? Vexed? Oh, very well, I don't mind, only you must settle it with Peggy. She's over there.

Something has gone wrong! Somebody hasn't come, or hasn't asked her to dance, when he did! Girls are so funny! It does not matter if a whole ball-room is at their feet—if the right man isn't. I wonder who it is? I could help her if she would tell me.

She won't. But for all her independence, she will come and cry on my shoulder to-night, and tell me it's oh, nothing!—but that she is perfectly, utterly, absolutely, hopelessly miserable! A mother is some good then!

XXIII

In Ned Tremaine's Studio in Chelsea.

MRS. FRED DEVEREL, surveying a portrait through a pince-nez.

It reminds me more of a Chéret poster than anything else. However . . . I don't know anything about it! (Despairingly.)

NED TREMAINE.

About what?

MRS. FRED DEVEREL.

Impressionism. Is that all you've done in ten sittings?

NED TREMAINE, moodily.

I'm not pleased with it myself. All you see there was done at the last sitting, and I shall probably paint it out again.

MRS. FRED DEVEREL.

All very well if you *did* paint it out, but I see five Modernas under this one.

NED TREMAINE, wearily.

C'est la vie! And the last shall be first.

MRS. FRED DEVEREL.

And what are all those streaks of red and blue in the background?

NED TREMAINE.

Don't you recognise it—a Lockhart's cocoa saloon? Miss Maskelyne is a modern young lady; I have painted

O

her in a London street, among all the shop-signs and posters and tokens of our modern civilisation. The cold blue of temperance, and the sensuous glow of butcher's meat . . . don't you see . . . ?

MRS. FRED DEVEREL.

Yes, I see—a combination up to date. Well, I must say Moderna is the least vain of women. Now, when *I* go to be painted—

NED TREMAINE.

You go to a first-rate bodice-and-skirt hand, warranted to turn out both corsage and face without wrinkle or crease! There are lots of artists like that. Here she comes! (To MODERNA.) Please pose yourself quickly. It's coming on very well, I think.

MODERNA.

May I look?

MRS. FRED DEVEREL.

Better not! (Aside.) Least *seen* is soonest mended—or forgiven.

MODERNA, looking at the picture.

Oh, Mr. Tremaine, are my lips the colour of sealing-wax, or of a soldier's uniform?

NED TREMAINE.

You remind me of the captious art critic, Miss Maskelyne. Those are the kind of unreasonable things they say.

For the critic's opinion, who has stultified himself with virtuous theories and righteous traditions, I have not the slightest regard; but you, who know absolutely nothing, I fondly believe, of the laws of art, are a critic not to be disdained. (MODERNA smiles.) Yes, you can give me that smile.

MODERNA.

No, I haven't read Vasari, but I have an opinion, and I am not sure you would agree with it.

NED TREMAINE.

Who may abuse one if not one's friends? (Becomes absorbed.)

MRS. FRED DEVEREL, suddenly.

I say, Moderna, will you excuse me a minute while I go round to De Chathuant's studio? I promised to look in, sometime, and see what he is doing. I'll only be a minute.— (MODERNA nods.) Exit Mrs. DEVEREL.

. NED TREMAINE.

Are you going to the next *En Avant* Social Evening, Miss Maskelyne?

MODERNA.

Of course. I am a member.

NED TREMAINE.

You go with my sister Dolly, don't you? It is very odd to see you there. " A snowy dove trooping with crows. . . ."

MODERNA.

That is not very polite to your sister.

NED TREMAINE.

Oh, Dolly is a law unto herself. She's neither dove nor crow, but a kind of literary bird of prey, seeking whom she may devour—and interview !

MODERNA.

Awfully clever people go to the Club; that's why I joined. One likes to keep pace with modern thought. They are so frankly pagan there. (Laughing.) At least the President of it told me that such was her ambition. . . .

NED TREMAINE.

Frankly "pot-house," I should say. Still it's amusing, and you are not obliged to soil your white wings. One *can* touch pitch and yet not be defiled, if one snubs it well. You see a poor devil like me has to go anywhere and everywhere, and tout for commissions, and see fellows who may be useful to him—

MODERNA.

And paint, too ! You are forgetting you are an artist, Mr. Tremaine.

NED TREMAINE.

Oh yes, I make my little experiments—

MODERNA.

On the patient public ?

NED TREMAINE.

We artists are all pilgrims, you know, in a strange land —adventurers—pioneers—

MODERNA, shyly.

I think if you took a little more pains . . .

NED TREMAINE, laughing.

Am I not always explaining to you that the first impact
of a scene on the visual organs is the essential; that all
detail ought to be subordinated to the flash of insight;
that any sense of effort would be fatal.   The picture
must come right at once or not come at all—it must
be seen and grasped in a flash—

MODERNA.

And seen and passed like a flash.   I propose a kind of
revolving picture gallery . . .

NED TREMAINE.

Ah, you're getting a little mixed . . .

MODERNA.

So would the critics !   Go on painting.   I won't talk.
(Composes her features.)   I hear the studio bell.

NED TREMAINE.

Perhaps it's Lord Coniston !   I'll see. . . .   No, it isn't.
He promised to come.   He's just back from that
infernal foolhardy yacht race of his . . . won it though !

MODERNA.

What is he coming here for ?

NED TREMAINE.

He's coming to see a portrait I've done. He is
interested in the sitter. He brought her here, and I
painted her in costume, by request, though it is not my
way.

MODERNA.

Who is it?

NED TREMAINE.

A Mrs. Belinfante . . . a Frenchwoman. . . . I used to
hear about her when I lived in Paris. A kind of beautiful
cosmopolitan creature—fur, cigarettes, diamonds—

MODERNA.

Oh, do you mean a person like that?

NED TREMAINE.

My dear Miss Maskelyne, she's rich enough to have her
own way, that's all I mean. She is *très bien vue* in Paris
—every one raves about her. Deuced clever woman!
They say Coniston is going to marry her!

MODERNA.

Why should he?

NED TREMAINE.

Don't know. He fought a duel about her once. He
compromised her—or she him, I forget which . . . She
had a husband then, a villain, who beat her . . .

MODERNA.

And he died . . . and her beauty and her misfortunes so
affected Lord Coniston that he is to marry her?

NED TREMAINE.

That's about it.   She's in London now.   She wants to
take her portrait back to Paris with her.

MODERNA.

Is it done?

NED TREMAINE.

It depends entirely how you look at it.   Coniston is
coming to decide at twelve.   It's a quarter to, now.

MODERNA.

Show!

NED TREMAINE.

I knew you would want to see it.

MODERNA.

Yes, please.

NED TREMAINE draws a canvas forward.

You see it is done in my old manner.

MODERNA, after a pause.

I wish you had done me like that.

NED TREMAINE.

Do you think her pretty?

MODERNA, enthusiastically.

Lovely!

NED TREMAINE, aside.

I like this girl.   She doesn't deny the woman's beauty, though she's deadly jealous of her, I can tell.   (Aloud.) Look, here is her dress !   A Marquise—Pompadour— paniers—ruffles—all the rest of it.

MODERNA.

She's just my height.

NED TREMAINE.

Rather like you, in fact.

MODERNA, suddenly.

What a time Flossie is !   I wish you would go and dig her out. . . .

NED TREMAINE.

I don't want her.

MODERNA, with hauteur.

But I do.   Please, go !

NED TREMAINE.

But if Coniston comes ?   It's his hour.

MODERNA.

I'll entertain him.   I know him, you know.

NED TREMAINE, aside.

I didn't know.   Confound that unruly member of mine !

Exit.

MODERNA, sola.

Edward has been in town three days, and not been to
see me yet. And I shall meet him. He will be
surprised. This woman—I wonder who she is? He
expects to see her here! Suppose I put on the *Marquise*
dress, and assume her attitude? Dare I? I should
like to give Edward a shock. It would be so dramatic.
I shall know on what terms . . . oh, he can't care for a
stagey woman like that! Lovely, she is, though. (Begins
to put the dress on.) If only he comes to time! He will.
He was always so punctual, that was one of the
things that bored me so about him. . . . The dress
actually fits—over my other! She is stout, I suppose.
(Poses herself.) Only I want a fan, paint, and powder, and
impudence to complete the costume. I hear the bell!
The old woman will open. . . . I can't think why I'm
trembling so. . . .

Enter Lord CONISTON. She stiffens her features.

CONISTON.

Why—Elise!

MODERNA, drily.

Do you call her Elise, then? (Comes down from the estrade.)
How do you do? Help me off with this before Flossie
and Mr. Tremaine come back. (Feverishly unfastening the dress.)

CONISTON, slowly.

Yes. . . . How do you do. . . . But why have you put
on Mrs. Belinfante's costume?

MODERNA.

Because I was a malicious fool. Never mind, my weapon has turned against myself. . . .

CONISTON, coldly.

I don't understand you. . . .

MODERNA.

All the better. (Leaning against a chair.)

CONISTON.

Are you faint ? You look quite pale.

MODERNA.

It's with sitting. . . . Here comes Flossie. Now I can go.

Re-enter Mrs. FRED DEVEREL and NED TREMAINE. They both shake hands
with Lord CONISTON.

NED TREMAINE.

Sorry I was away, but I hope Miss Maskelyne did the honours.

CONISTON.

Indeed, yes ; she even got up a little *scena* for my benefit. (Putting up his glass, and looking at MODERNA's portrait.) A—Tremaine—what a delightful disregard of detail !

MRS. FRED DEVEREL, to MODERNA, aside.

My dear girl, what is it ? You look quite yellow. . . .

MODERNA.

Let's go, please, Flossie. I can't sit any more to-day. (To CONISTON, stiffly.) I am so glad you have come home. Will you be my guest at the *soirée* of the *En Avant* Club to-morrow night?

CONISTON.

I shall be very happy.

MODERNA.

I'll send you a card. Good-bye. Good-bye, Mr. Tremaine. I will write to you when I can come again, and Flossie can manage it. Give Dolly my love, and say I'll call for her and take her to the Club to-morrow night.

Exit with Mrs. FRED DEVEREL.

XXIV

AT the En Avant Club. A mixed social evening. MODERNA and DOLLY TREMAINE on the stairs.

MODERNA.

I say, Dolly, can't you leave that book in the rack?

DOLLY TREMAINE.

No, dear, I'm afraid not. It's so improper I must stick to it. (Looking closely at MODERNA.) Why, how respectable you look in your pure white dress — almost dignified ! I can't think why you always dress so primly at our social evenings?

MODERNA.

Perhaps I do it on purpose ?

DOLLY TREMAINE.

Well, you look sweet anyhow; come on ! I see Ned over there looking like a saint — my brother's worth a hundred pounds to me, any day, in respectability.   He is so brilliantly ugly.   Oh and Moderna, I must introduce you to my little editor, sometime.   He's dying to know you.

MODERNA.

What for ?

DOLLY TREMAINE.

He probably wants to ask you to write for him.

MODERNA.

Nonsense !

DOLLY TREMAINE.

It's your name he wants.   You're nuts to him.   You see, you have the *entrée* into all sorts of fashionable society . . .

MODERNA.

How hatefully you talk, Dolly !

DOLLY TREMAINE.

It's business.   There he is !   Won't I just bully him for the way he mauled my article on " 'Bus-tops." (They enter a room full of people and smoke.)

*   *   *   *   *

DE CHATHUANT.

Tiens, la jolie philosophe—and her familiar spirit !

MRS. FRED DEVEREL.

Why do you call her that ?

DE CHATHUANT.

Parce qu'elle discute si joliment sur des choses dont elle ne comprend rien—heureusement !   Pour l'autre, je ne dis pas !

MRS. FRED DEVEREL.

Oh, D. T. and her music hall refrains are getting too much even for me !   She leaves *fin de siècle* far behind. It's the beginning of the one after next with her. How do you do, Miss Tremaine.   Are you going to dance the *chahut* in that short frock ?

DE CHATHUANT, to MODERNA.

Bon soir, Mademoiselle.   Quelle toilette !   Blanche comme une fée !

MRS. FRED DEVEREL.

Except for those malign-looking flowers.   What are they?

MODERNA.

Fritillaries.   I rather like these poisonous colours, don't you ?

DE CHATHUANT.

Un ange qui porte les Fleurs du Mal !   Cette mise fantastique vous sied admirablement.   When will you come and let me 'ave a croquis ?

MODERNA, doubtfully.

I don't know . . . You say I mustn't bring a chaperon ?

DE CHATHUANT.

Ah, pour ça, non, mille fois non ! Can I work with a British matron at my elbow ? The inspiration would leave me . . . paf !

MODERNA.

I'll bring William some day when he comes up from Eton.

DE CHATHUANT.

Un garçon—diable ! Merci, Mademoiselle, je préfère le croquis du souvenir.

MRS. FRED DEVEREL.

I'll bring her some day, Monsieur de Chathuant. (Aside to MODERNA.) You mustn't snub a genius like that, you little idiot ! Don't you want your picture in the Salon ?

MODERNA, pettishly.

I'm tired of sitting to people !

MRS. FRED DEVEREL.

Take care, dear, you're getting spoilt ! Talk to Mr. Tremaine ; he has been waiting at your elbow for an age. (To Miss TREMAINE.) Well, Miss Dolly, where have *you* come from—" with all your love locks flowing—— "

DOLLY TREMAINE.

And "vine leaves in my hair"—

MRS. FRED DEVEREL.

Some East End doss-house—or an opium den—or some other low resort of copy?

DOLLY TREMAINE, cheerfully.

The East End is rather played out. I think I shall begin to turn my attention to the low-lived deeps of the Upper Ten. Slumming at Belvoir! Coster courtship of lady 'Liza Vere de Vere and Lord Henry——? Wouldn't it just sound novel? For the present I've come from behind the scenes at the Vanities. Tilly Drew was fine in that new song of hers *You don't draw me!* You know, poor girl, she can't manage to get up steam to sing it at all now, unless she has a B and S first. She's as sorry as any one, but she can't do without.

MRS. FRED DEVEREL, sneering.

Talent obliges!

DOLLY TREMAINE.

I wish I had been there last night! She had a lovely row with Bessie Bannister—they call Tilly and Bessie "the cat" and "the devil," at the theatre, you know! Well, here it is; Bessie contrives to stick her foot out in the third act, when Tilly's dance is on and she wants the whole stage to herself. Tilly has threatened to speak to the management if it occurs again, but Bessie

goes on doing it, and last night Tilly went up to her
and said aloud " You—You—You "—

MRS. FRED DEVEREL.

Words failed her.

DOLLY TREMAINE.

At first, but . . . (Shakes her head.)

MRS. FRED DEVEREL.

Who is Moderna talking to, over there, with a head like
a burning bush ?

DOLLY TREMAINE.

That is Maurice Kronofski—he wrote the " Devils'
Chorus," you know—and oh, there is Gontram Vere?
the new poet—*Flies in Amber*, don't you know ? I
am to interview him for the *Blowfly*, am I not, Mr.
Spofforth ? (To the Editor of the *Blowfly*, who approaches.)

THE EDITOR, shortly.

Will you make me known to your friend Miss Maskelyne.

DOLLY TREMAINE.

'Pleasure ! . . . (Performs the ceremony and turns to GONTRAM VERE.)
You know I am to have the pleasure of interviewing
you ?

GONTRAM VERE.

Yes, but first tell me, who is that young lady on your
right ?

DOLLY TREMAINE, aside.

Now, if I were of the feminine persuasion, how jealous I should be. It's lucky I am of the neuter gender. (Aloud.) My friend, Miss Maskelyne. She's going in for journalism.

GONTRAM VERE.

Under your auspices? How delightful I I am constantly seeing the familiar initials D. T. in our leading periodicals. By the way, I used to know Miss Maskelyne—I am afraid to say how long ago.

DOLLY TREMAINE.

Do you think she has altered?

GONTRAM VERE.

Well, she had hardly so much *aplomb*. . . . Who is she talking to now?

DOLLY TREMAINE.

My brother.

GONTRAM VERE.

Is that your brother?

DOLLY TREMAINE.

Yes, doesn't he look good—and ugly?

GONTRAM VERE.

Shall I say, the exact opposite of his sister?

DOLLY TREMAINE, delighted.

Yes, I flatter myself *I'm* like the girl in the song. " Not

P

too good," etc.   I hate your hardened saints.   Do come
and have a sandwich. . . .

*   *   *   *   *

MODERNA, to NED TREMAINE.

He asked me to write him society paragraphs.

NED TREMAINE.

Well !

MODERNA.

And I said I couldn't—and he said : oh, just jot down
my impressions of society, and he would pull them
straight in the office !   Fancy furnishing "spicy bits of
gossip," and making capital out of my friends !

NED TREMAINE.'

Dolly does it.

MODERNA.

But Dolly's friends seem to like it.   Mine wouldn't.

NED TREMAINE.

Most of Dolly's friends, you see, have to make their way
—as she has.

MODERNA.

Yes, I know, but I *couldn't* make a friend of a serio-
comic !

NED TREMAINE.

You've never even seen one, I suppose.   You ought to ;
it is a feature of the age.

MODERNA.

Dolly is always wanting to take me to a music hall.

NED TREMAINE.

Don't go with her. Go with me.

MODERNA.

Oh, I couldn't.

NED TREMAINE.

There you are! The conventional answer! Haven't I
heard you say a hundred times that you wanted to see—
to do everything—that a girl ought to be able to go
about the same as a man !

MODERNA.

But not *with* a man !

NED TREMAINE.

But I don't count, do I ?   I'm so hideous.

MODERNA, looking at him compassionately.

Well, perhaps I will some day, with you—and Dolly.

NED TREMAINE.

It would be much more proper to go alone with me.   I
am absolutely uncompromising, while Dolly—

GONTRAM VERE, interrupting.

Miss Maskelyne, I really must re-introduce myself to
you. You remember me ?

MODERNA.

Of course I do.

GONTRAM VERE.

I have been to India, and America, and Australia, since I saw you. Oh, those days at Merrow! I shall never forget them. Have you?

MODERNA.

I have been reading your book. It reminded me of them.

GONTRAM VERE.

How good of you! What do you think of it? Abuse it if you would like. A little adverse criticism would be so pleasant. Who may abuse a man if not his friends? But tell me—I am nothing if not transitional—what have you been doing? I saw some verses of yours in a journal the other day. Do you throw off these little gem-like effusions in the intervals of arranging those wonderful toilettes? (Looking at her.) How I remember the simple little gown in which I saw you first!

MODERNA, laughing.

I have altered since then.

GONTRAM VERE.

You were like a Botticelli, now you are like a Greuze— a lily, and now a rose. . . .

MODERNA, curtly.

I've grown up; that's all!

GONTRAM VERE.

But I'm not sure that I did not love the old Moderna Maskelyne the best.   The shy, spiritual child, with eyes of wonder. . . . Do you remember a sonnet I once wrote to you?

MODERNA, blushing.

Yes.

GONTRAM VERE.

How did it run?   Ah, you can't remember!   Strangely enough, nor can I?   But I am bringing out a new edition of my poems—and I should be glad to include it.

MODERNA.

I'm afraid—

GONTRAM VERE.

Is it too personal?   I can modify it. . . .

MODERNA.

Not at all, only.   . . (Aside.)   I've torn it up!   (Aloud.) Will you introduce me to your wife?

GONTRAM VERE.

Poor child, she's so shy. . . . Praise my work, Miss Maskelyne, if you want to put her at her ease.   Come here, Melilot darling, and let me introduce you to Miss Maskelyne.

MODERNA, politely.

I've just been reading your husband's last article, in the *Incontrovertible*, Mrs. Vere.   I tell him it is a shocking waste of sonnets.

MRS. VERE, earnestly.

Oh, there are no rhymes in it, I hope, are there, Gon-tram?   That would be dreadful.

MODERNA.

When are we to have another, Mr. Vere?

GONTRAM VERE, wearily passing his hand through his hair.

I do not know, I am sure.   It is a matter for serious consideration. . . . I don't want, you know, to be flogged with my own laurels. . . .

MRS. VERE.

Flogged, Gontram?

GONTRAM VERE.

Go and have a sandwich, dear, with Mr. Saintfoin, who asks you.   (She goes.)   What do you think of my wife?

MODERNA.

She is very good-looking.

GONTRAM VERE.

Indubitably.   In everything else, she is my exact opposite.   She is as domestic as I am nomadic.   She is my good angel and keeps me straight—my accounts, you know.   She was an orphan when I met her, under the most touching circumstances.   I first saw her in her insignia of grief—tenderly outlined against a pink background of butcher's meat—she was choosing a chop for her invalid father.   It moved me at once. . . . But

I must not monopolise you.   There is an extraordinarily
handsome man who has been glowering at me for the
last quarter of an hour.   He will assassinate me if I
talk to you any longer.   (Goes.)

MODERNA, aside.

Yes, he looks a prince among all these people.   (Aloud to
Lord Coniston.)   So you have come !

CONISTON.

You invited me.

MODERNA.

It was nice of you.   (Nervously.)   I hope you know somebody here ?

CONISTON.

Only that clever old fellow over there—De Chathuant.
Whose guest is he ?

MODERNA, triumphantly.

Miss Tremaine's !

CONISTON, mildly.

I must present my respects to Miss Tremaine.   I see
she is talking to that man Caffrey.

MODERNA.

Who is Caffrey ?

CONISTON.

Oh, a very pleasant creature—a journalist, and a black-
mailer, and all that sort of thing. . . .

MODERNA, angrily.

Edward, I won't stand it.

CONISTON, innocently.

What won't you stand? And why are you not smoking?

MODERNA, reproachfully.

You know I never do.

CONISTON.

I don't know. I've been so long away. Besides every one seems to smoke here. Have they all nerves?

MODERNA.

If you come here just to sneer at my friends . . .

CONISTON.

I didn't know they were your friends. Mr. Caffrey can't be your friend. I did not come here to sneer at any one; I came to see you, and I shall do my best to see nobody else.

MODERNA.

That means to say that you think them inferior . . .

CONISTON, gravely.

Don't let us discuss them. Tell me about yourself, that is, if you can really think it worth while to talk to an outsider like myself. I am merely a private person. I can neither offer to immortalise you in the New English Art Club, nor give you the Ladies' Column in the *Blowfly* to do, nor—

MODERNA.

Oh, Edward, how narrow you are! How intolerant! How insulting! Don't you see these are real men and women, a thousand times more interesting than the stiff, silly, idle mashers, and empty-headed women one meets in drawing-rooms, who can only talk gossip and clothes and parties—

CONISTON.

Every class talks its own shop!

MODERNA.

They are perhaps a little rough and ready, and they call things by their right names, but they are the people that make the world go round, . . . who affect millions through the press . . . they are the levers that move the world. . . .

CONISTON.

That's just it—they are *not* the real levers. Do you suppose that there are not backwaters of literature and journalism where the scum collects, and curdles, and fumes, and eddies,—quite useless as far as the further-ance of the world is concerned——

MODERNA, laughing.

That is quite good copy, though the metaphor's a little mixed, and you are excessively unfair. I know you hate Bohemians. You always did.

CONISTON, earnestly.

I do *not* hate Bohemians—not the real, half-starved,

half-clothed Bohemian, who has no friends, and no visiting cards, and no dress clothes to go out in—nothing, but the touch of genius which makes him come to the top.

MODERNA.

Yes, you would have patronised Johnson, as Lord Southampton patronised Shakespeare !—I know.

CONISTON.

—But I have nothing but scorn for the men who have every attribute of Bohemia but its genius, who glory in never answering a letter or keeping an engagement, and clog the wheels of the world by their impertinent want of punctuality—the men whose word isn't their bond, who considers the phrase *c'etait plus fort que moi* an excuse for breaking every law human and divine. . . . I don't suppose there is one man in the room with the most rudimentary sense of conscience . . . and to see you masquerading here among them, like the Lady in Comus ! . . . and there is that brute and cad Caffrey over there, and I'm hanged, Moderna, if I'll stay another minute in the same room with him.   Good-night ! Forgive me. . . . I'll see you to-morrow night at the Flemings.

MODERNA, drily.

I don't think you will.   Good-night.   (Exit CONISTON. To NED TREMAINE, breathlessly.)   Mr. Tremaine, I'll go with you to a music-hall to-morrow night.   Get Dolly.

NED TREMAINE.

She's going to a rehearsal. . . .

MODERNA.

Very well, then—with you, alone. ₁Write to me and
arrange it. No, I'll write to you. Good-night. I can't
wait for Dolly. No, please, I am *never* seen home. It
is a principle. Good-night.

XXV

IN Kensington Gardens, about seven o'clock, on a summer evening.

MODERNA.

Oh, this is perfectly hateful! Which seat did I say?
There must be a mistake. This is the first assignation
I ever made, and I'm here first! It is too humili-
ating! . . .

Suppose I go a little way off and come up out of
breath? No; that would look as if I were in a hurry
to meet him. How dare he be late? It's excessively
rude! (Looks at her watch.) Oh, I see, I am too early—it
was because I was so nervous, and so afraid of Peggy
catching me. I'll sit down for five minutes, and if he
isn't here exactly to the minute, I'll go back.

I'd give anything to go back now, but I am not going
to be domineered over by Edward. But as for enjoying
it . . . I shall feel perfectly miserable all the time. I
had much better have gone to the Flemings. I shall
cut it as short as I can. Let me see, . . . my people
are going on to three things after the Blakes' dinner.
They will not be back for ages. I shall be home and

tucked up in bed by the time they come—long before!
I shall stay no longer with Ned Tremaine than is consistent with politeness.

Here comes a policeman! How he looks at me!
Oh, I am not doing anything wrong! He'll tell me to
move on in a minute. I will . . . No, he's gone the
other way. And anyhow, I don't see how he *could* stop
me sitting on a bench in Kensington Gardens. I'm not
"spoiling the shrubs and the flowers."

Suppose one of our servants should come by? They
come here to meet their sweethearts, naturally. That is
what I seem to be doing.

Ned Tremaine!!

Oh, this is killing me. I'll go home, and send a
wire to him. . . .   (Rises, and gathers up her skirts in a resolute knot,
and turns away, just as NED TREMAINE comes up.)

NED TREMAINE.

Miss Maskelyne!   ·

MODERNA, turning round, very calmly.

Dear me, is that you, Mr. Tremaine?

NED TREMAINE.

Who else should it be? I am so sorry you got here
first. (Looking at his watch.)   I never knew a woman so
more than punctual. I always time myself to be five
minutes before. . . .

MODERNA.

You speak as if you were in the habit of keeping
appointments. . . . (Aside.)   Oh dear, I wish I hadn't said
that.

NED TREMAINE.

Ah, now you are cross because I wasn't here first!

MODERNA, aside.

Cross! How dare he say I am cross! (Aloud.) Oh, it doesn't matter. . . .

NED TREMAINE.

But it does matter. I hurried to be here five minutes before you, and I am so disappointed. Tell me, how long *did* you wait?

MODERNA.

Oh, please, Mr. Tremaine, don't say any more about it. I said I'd go to a music hall with you, and I will. Can we get a hansom?

NED TREMAINE.

No difficulty. We'll walk to one if you don't mind. Well, about our Bohemian dinner? I thought we would go to Nick's—I mean Nicolini's.

MODERNA.

Is it very Bohemian? I think I should like it as low as possible.

NED TREMAINE.

Quite low enough for you to start with. I'll give you a real Italian dinner. It is an experience. They will do anything for me there. Then we'll get a copy of the *Entr'Acte*, and see where the best turns are. I think the Tivoli. We'll have a box.

MODERNA.

No, I don't want to be in a box.   I want to sit with the people.

'NED TREMAINE.

People with a big P !   Are you a socialist ?   Well, we'll do exactly as you like ; only in a box you can sit back, you know..

MODERNA.

I don't want to sit back, I am not ashamed.   (Aside.) What an awful lie !   (They get into a hansom. He supports her elbow with his hand.)

MODERNA, suddenly.

Will you tell him to stop at the nearest telegraph office ? I want to send a wire—to my dressmaker.

NED TREMAINE.

An urgent appeal to postpone cutting the bodice till further instructions ?   Blue bows instead of white ? . . .

MODERNA.

I see you know all about it, Mr. Tremaine.

NED TREMAINE.

Portrait painter, you know ! . . .   Here is the office. Shall I send the wire for you ?

MODERNA, getting out.

No.   What music hall did we settle to go to ?

NED TREMAINE.

We didn't settle, exactly.

MODERNA.

Yes, we did ; the Tivoli. (They go into the Post Office. MODERNA scribbles a message, and hands it to the clerk.)

THE CLERK.

How do you spell this name, miss ?

MODERNA.

C—o—n . . . oh, it's all right. I wrote it quite clearly. (To TREMAINE.) Now let us go. Are you sure I look plain enough ?

NED TREMAINE.

Not half plain enough.

MODERNA, impatiently

I mean my clothes.

NED TREMAINE.

Oh, your dress ! . . . That bonnet is a masterpiece of discretion !

MODERNA.

And my veil ? I've two on, I wish I had three.

NED TREMAINE.

"Through a veil darkly." This sudden horror of publicity is not quite consistent with your previous remarks, Miss Maskelyne.

MODERNA, pettishly.

Why should I be consistent? (They alight at NICOLINI'S. NED
TREMAINE orders a dinner.)

*   *   *   *   *

NED TREMAINE.

How do you like an Italian dinner, Miss Maskelyne?

MODERNA.

I thought it was a Bohemian one.   Very good indeed.
I didn't expect . . .   But this place is so smart—and
quite clean.   Is it really like that place you go to in
Paris . . . the Chat Noir, or the Rat Mort, or whatever
it is?

NED TREMAINE.

Well, no—not exactly . . . but it is very good for a beginning.   We must not shock you at first.   Well, and
where shall we go?   I see Cissie Loftus is indisposed.
Would you rather go to the Pavilion?

MODERNA.

'Oh no, *no ;* I've set my heart on the Tivoli.

NED TREMAINE.

But isn't it a pity when Cissie is not on?

MODERNA.

I didn't come for any particular star.   I came—for the
experience.

NED TREMAINE.

And how do you like it—the experience, so far?

MODERNA, aside.

Poor man, he's giving me my dinner. (Aloud.) It is
delightful, Mr. Tremaine, but . . . I don't feel as if it
would have done me any harm to have a chaperon about !

NED TREMAINE.

It depends on the chaperon. A skilled and trained
chaperon is very difficult to procure. A really nice one
is worth her weight—in compliments. Dolly has long
since given it up as a bad business. I say, do have
some of this Zambulione !

MODERNA.

It's so sticky—and these veils are so hot—and I am
so afraid of eating through them, and if I turn them up
it makes a hard line over my nose !

NED TREMAINE.

Il faut souffrir pour être Bohémienne. You are dreadfully timorous now. Next time you come you will only
have one veil, and the next after that—none !

MODERNA.

Next time I come ! . . . What o'clock is it ?

NED TREMAINE.

Time to go. *Allons !* (Offers to help her on with her cape.) How
independent you are !
They go. The cab draws up in front of the Tivoli.

NED TREMAINE, getting out.

Wait in the cab, will you, please, while I get a box ?
Q

We *must* have a box this time, at any rate.   Why are
you looking round so anxiously ?

MODERNA.

To see if there is any one I know.

NED TREMAINE, going in.

Prudent child !

MODERNA.

That is the last straw !   (Leans out of the hansom, and beckons to
Lord CONISTON, who is standing stiffly in the porch.)   Oh, Edward, you
got my wire ?   You'll take care of me, won't you ?

CONISTON.

I will ; but you must manage it yourself.

MODERNA.

Yes, I'll manage it ; only stand by me.   Here he is !

NED TREMAINE, coming back.

How do, Coniston ?   Now, Miss Maskelyne, get out.
Here we are, a nice little cosy box—

MODERNA.

I'm so sorry, Mr. Tremaine, but . . . I've got a dreadful
headache, and . . . I don't want to spoil your evening
. . . so I have asked Lord Coniston to take me home.
I hope you will forgive me . . . I'm very sorry, but I'm
sure you will understand . . .

NED TREMAINE, with studied politeness.

I quite understand, Miss Maskelyne. You have turned faint-hearted about "the experience." At any rate, you have dined with me at Nicolini's—that will be something to remember! Good-night!

Exit.

CONISTON.

That was a nasty one. Have you deserved it? What does it all mean? How do you happen to be going about with this—gentleman? You sent for me, and I came . . . but, upon my word, I can't imagine what on earth you are about?

MODERNA.

Oh, don't ask me to explain. I was an idiot.

CONISTON.

Yes, but how did you?—

MODERNA.

I don't want to enter into particulars. I only know I'll never do it again. I never felt so miserably uncomfortable in my whole life.

CONISTON.

Did he?—

MODERNA.

Oh no, he behaved all right according to his lights . . . It was my fault. I got myself into a hole, and I have asked you to get me out. That's all, and thank you!

CONISTON.

It isn't all. He is a beastly little cad to even propose to take a young lady alone to . . .

MODERNA.

I made him, I tell you. . . . Don't let us bother with poor Ned Tremaine any more. He's really so dreadfully ugly that I thought he wouldn't matter. There's an end of it! Are you not going to take me in?

CONISTON.

Take you in? Into the music-hall? Do the very thing I am abusing him for?

MODERNA.

You are different, Edward.

CONISTON, laughing.

I hope so . . . but still I don't mean to do it. (To the cabman.) 280 Queen's Gate. (Gets in beside her.) I'm going to take you home. . . .

MODERNA.

I wish I hadn't sent for you. . . . (Sulks.)

XXVI

In the Maskelynes' drawing-room. Tea-time.

BILLY DANVERS, taking up his hat.

Well, I must be off. I promised to call on Flossie Deverel. Are you coming to Bleahope for the hunting?

MODERNA.

Yes, for a fortnight; after my people have gone abroad.

BILLY DANVERS.

Oh, ah . . . yes . . . and when do they go?

MODERNA.

Next week.

BILLY DANVERS.

And you have really, seriously decided not to go with
them to the Riviera?

MODERNA.

Yes, really, seriously.

BILLY DANVERS.

By Jove, I think you must be—

MODERNA.

A fool.   Say so!

BILLY DANVERS.

Well, if you ask me, it seems to me perfectly idiotic that
a girl can't manage to live comfortably with her people
and get on with them.

MODERNA.

A man never can.   Why don't you live in Mount Street
with your father and your mother?

BILLY DANVERS.

A man is different.

MODERNA, scornfully.

The usual answer ! ·

BILLY DANVERS.

He is quite different. He's got a profession . . . he has got friends . . . he wants to go about freely without being asked a lot of beastly questions.

MODERNA.

So does a girl.

BILLY DANVERS.

Rot! She doesn't really want; and if she does, she oughtn't to. It won't do. I tell you, *I* know. You women all screech for your liberty; and when you have got it, you don't know what to do with it. You swagger about standing alone and all that, and yet you want a fuss made about you all the time. How you would come down on a man if he did not look after you, and offer you his arm, and all that sort of thing !

MODERNA.

That is mere ordinary politeness.

BILLY DANVERS.

One man doesn't open the door for another. It's only because you're women and weak we do it . . . and we ought to leave off the moment you all get so deuced independent. I think women are getting horrid nowadays—nearly all. . . . I only hope there'll be some nice little girl saved for me out of the general wreck when I marry — well-groomed, well-chaperoned, well looked after. . . . And who is going to chaperon you

while they are away?   Are you going to have Aunt
Eliza to stay with you?

MODERNA.

They have let the house for four months.

BILLY DANVERS.

The deuce they have!   And where are you going to
put up?

MODERNA.

I'm going to share her flat with—I think you know
her—Miss Dolly Tremaine.

BILLY DANVERS.

I know her; yes, in a sort of way.   Everybody knows
her!   Oh, you can't; you absolutely can't chum up with
D. T.   Every one will drop you; take my word for it.

MODERNA.

She is quite, quite respectable.

BILLY DANVERS.

I daresay she is; so is the housemaid.   What has that
to do with it?   But she's an out-and-out Bohemian—
she isn't in society.   Don't do it.   Nobody will call on
you; nobody—

MODERNA.

The clergyman of the parish will, at any rate.

BILLY DANVERS.

Mr. Brown.   He's in love with you, poor creature!   And

you are actually giving up three months on the Riviera
to go and live in Bohemia with that deplorable girl?

MODERNA.

I *never* want to leave London, you know.

BILLY DANVERS.

But London in the winter !   And there is such delightful
society abroad just now.   Oh, you will never make me
believe there isn't some very strong motive for your
wanting to stay in town . . . something, or somebody. . . .

MODERNA, after a pause.

I am not trying to make you believe anything, Billy. . . .
I think you had better go now.   I expect Miss Tremaine
every moment ; and after what you have said of her, I
don't suppose you are anxious to meet her. . . . Good-bye
. . . I am not cross.

BILLY goes.   Miss TREMAINE is announced.

DOLLY TREMAINE, boisterously.

Well, dear, and is it all settled?   Have you triumphed?

MODERNA, gloomily.

Yes, I have triumphed.

DOLLY.

Was there an awful row?

MODERNA.

Yes ; we all spoke of nothing else for three days . . .

the last three days we have not spoken at all. I am in disgrace, but I am going to do as I choose. . . .

DOLLY.

Of course you are. You are a grown-up woman. No one has any right to control you. I knew the moment you chose to put your foot down, that they couldn't stand out. It was an infamous plan. The idea of dragging *you*, one of the most brilliant women in London, abroad, and burying you alive for three months. No, I said, directly I heard of it, Moderna must not desert her sphere. . . .

MODERNA.

What *is* my sphere, Dolly?

DOLLY.

The sphere—our sphere—the sphere of the people who really live, and think, and feel, and enjoy life, and drink its cup to the dregs. Oh, what a time we will have, I and you! We will go everywhere, and see everything, and hear everything, and be in it—right in it—up to our little chins—in the stream of life. It will be delightful!

MODERNA, spiritlessly.

Delightful!

DOLLY.

And we will have jolly little unconventional suppers up in my flat, you know, and ask all the new people. You shall ask your men, and I shall ask mine. We will get Maurice Kronofski to come and play his maddest music to us; and we will have Gontram Vere . . . mustn't have his wife, I think, she'd spoil it! And there's a delightful Anarchist come to live on the third floor—

MODERNA, sarcastically.

He can bring us his bombs to play with !

DOLLY.

And Ned is invaluable. By the way he is cross with you. He says you played it rather low down on him about the music hall the other day. He says he didn't believe you had a headache at all, you simply wanted to go off with Lord Coniston. I don't much care for your friend Coniston, you know,—he snubs me—but I shan't object to your asking him to the suppers, of course. There's nothing mean about me !

MODERNA.

No, dear. (Aside.) I don't seem to see Edward there, though, with Kronofski—and Vere—and a murderer. . . . He would not come, even if I did ask him. (Aloud.) It all sounds very nice, but . . .

DOLLY.

Yes ; and now we must discuss finances. I have been making inquiries. The rent of the extra room is nothing, you can easily do it out of your allowance. It will only mean a dress or two the less. . . .

MODERNA.

Yes, I planned it all out; I can easily do it out of my dress allowance, . . . but . . . it's dreadful, Dolly. . . .

DOLLY.

You mean they have cut off your allowance? Never mind, dear. (Impulsively.) I'll finance you. I must have you with me at any price.

MODERNA.

Thank you, dear; I know you would be nice . . . but that isn't it. . . . Poor mother . . .

DOLLY.

Well, poor mother—?

MODERNA.

She hates my doing it . . . you know . . . and yet . . . isn't it dreadful? . . . she went to father, and she spoke to him . . . and asked him to forgive me . . . and she made him write me a cheque for £100, and she gave it me, and kissed me . . . and said she could not bear to think of my not having all I wanted and had been accustomed to—and would that do for four months?

DOLLY.

Magnificent!

MODERNA.

And she hoped that I should . . . that my experiment would be as successful as I expected, and . . .

DOLLY.

Rosamond and the Purple Jar all over again!

MODERNA.

But, Dolly, are you not touched? It was heaping coals of fire on me—I—

DOLLY.

It was turning the tables on you very cleverly. Regular *cliché* of the situation—the natural development of the maternal instinct! Good old mother!

MODERNA.

It makes me feel that I ought to throw it all up, and go with them.

DOLLY.

That's what she did it for. Safe draw! All known methods failed! I should not have believed her to be so astute!

MODERNA.

Don't, Dolly.

A Pause.

DOLLY.

Well, old girl, what are you thinking about so deeply? I must go in a moment—now, in fact. It's all settled, isn't it. Good-bye.

MODERNA.

Yes, it's all settled, Dolly; I am very sorry to play you false, but I am going to tell my mother that I am willing to go abroad with her on Tuesday.

DOLLY.

You cannot be so weak!

MODERNA.

I wonder how you can be so hard.   It frightened me.

DOLLY.

I retract all my sarcastic remarks about mothers in general Won't that do?

MODERNA.

No, dear.   Give up the idea.   I *must* offer to go with them.   I *cannot* be so hateful, when they are so kind.

DOLLY, after a pause.

Look here, I'm off home.   I'm not going to bother you any more now; but write to me to-night, and say what you are going to do.

MODERNA, stolidly.

I have told you what I am going to do.

DOLLY, kissing her.

Obstinate little thing !   I don't for one moment imagine that you mean to throw me over.   You will think better of it.   You know (smiling) you will never be able to make up your mind to leave London, when it comes to the point.   *Au revoir !*   I shall see you again to-day.

Exit.

MODERNA.

Billy said that too. . . . I wonder why I do so hate the idea of leaving London?

*   *   *   *   *

At Miss Tremaine's rooms, an hour later.   Enter Moderna.

MODERNA.

Which is to be my room.   (Sits down and bursts into tears.)

DOLLY.

What is it, dear?

MODERNA.

I'm coming to live with you. . . . It serves me right.
. . . They . . . they won't take me with them now,
even if I want to!

XXVII

At Bleahope Hall, in Foxshire.   The Meet of the Foxshire Hounds.

MRS. FRED DEVEREL, to her husband.

Sir Henry Graham wants you, Fred! . . . I say, Moderna,
do be civil to George Provis.   You have no idea what
a lot they think of him about here.

MODERNA.

He seems a cad to me.

MRS. FRED DEVEREL.

Never mind.   All swells are cads, if you read the
divorce cases.   But one needn't have much to do with
them even if one does marry them—if one's as clever
as you are.   Don't let Violet Fleming and her mother
get him.   I have told Provis that you are considered

the cleverest girl in London, pretty—he sees that—
agreeable—when you like—that you dance like an angel,
and go to hounds like a bird—

MODERNA, laughing.

Quite necessary, that last qualification !

MRS. FRED DEVEREL.

Well, yes, in a hunting county like this, and Captain
Provis is always in the first flight and thinks no end
of himself. It is lucky that you do ride well, so few
London girls keep it up. Look here, Moderna, joking
apart, you have been going about a long time, and you
have made nothing of it, so far ; try to look at the thing
practically. I assure you all the girls about here would
give their eyes for George Provis of Hetherland to propose to them, and *you* have only to raise your little
finger . . . why, Arthur said, only yesterday—

MODERNA.

Arthur ? . . . (Aside.) She *is* so afraid of my making it
up with Arthur. . . .

MRS. FRED DEVEREL.

No, not Arthur—Coniston—was it ?

MODERNA, drily.

Well, what did *he* say ?

MRS. FRED DEVEREL.

Oh, Coniston is a thorough man of the world ; he would
think you, or any girl, an awful fool to refuse a magnificent position, and all that. We had a long, long talk
in the morning-room yesterday, all about you.

MODERNA.

What, all about me ?   Did my poor concerns—

MRS. FRED DEVEREL, bridling a little.

Not *all* about you, I must confess.   Poor Coniston!
In spite of that fashionable reserve of his, he is so
touchingly communicative when one gets him to oneself!   I believe in tête-a-têtes, don't you ?

Exit.

Captain PROVIS approaches.

MODERNA, aside.

So you leave me to one with this dreadful man Provis!
You think he will propose, and I shall accept, and
you'll have Edward all to yourself to flirt with.   I don't
care how much you flirt with Edward ; but, all the same,
I won't play your game.   I'll play one of my own, and
it *will* amuse them all so at dinner to-night when I tell
them.   " A good   seat an indispensable qualification."
Very well !   (Aloud.)   Good morning, Captain Provis.

CAPTAIN PROVIS.

So, Miss Maskelyne, you have come to see what Foxshire can do ?

MODERNA, blandly.

Yes, I thought I should like a ride, so I asked the
coachman to pick out a horse for me, and . . .

CAPTAIN PROVIS.

Coachman ?   Horse ?   You've got Selima.   I know her
of old.   I thought Fred had sold her.   You look a
perfect picture on her, Miss Maskelyne.

MODERNA.

Wait till I move ! . . . I'm a terrible duffer, Captain Provis, you know.

CAPTAIN PROVIS, smiling.

Hardly, I should think ! Why the way you sit your mare— ?

MODERNA, beginning to slouch.

I suppose I sit too upright ?

CAPTAIN PROVIS.

Rather not !

MODERNA.

How sweet and peaceful all the dogs do look, wagging their little tails !

CAPTAIN PROVIS.

Dogs ? Don't you mean hounds—or is that what they say in the Shires ?

MODERNA.

What shires ?

CAPTAIN PROVIS.

Why—oh, it doesn't matter !

The hounds are thrown into covert.

MODERNA.

What a fuss the—what do you call them ?—hounds are making !

CAPTAIN PROVIS.

There's a fox at home, I fancy, but he declines to leave his lodgings.

R

MODERNA, naïvely.

Oh, then he will be minced in covert? I've got that right, haven't I?

CAPTAIN PROVIS.

My dear young lady, don't say minced.

MODERNA.

Hashed then.   I know it is hashed.

CAPTAIN PROVIS.

Oh, please, say chopped.

MODERNA.

Ah! I knew it was something they do in kitchens.

There is a general rush.

CAPTAIN PROVIS.

Jove!   Come on!   He's making straight for Ford.

MODERNA.

Heavens! what a pace!

CAPTAIN PROVIS.

Yes, rather a cracker.

MODERNA, breathlessly.

My beast's pulling so.   I can't manage it; I can't, really.

CAPTAIN PROVIS.

Give her her head, for heaven's sake!

MODERNA.

And there's an awful fence coming! I shall never get over it . . . oh, dear . . .

CAPTAIN PROVIS.

It's nothing when you come to it.

MODERNA.

I can't help it, I'm going round by the gate. Don't mind me.

CAPTAIN PROVIS, aside.

Confound. . . . Lost my place. (Aloud.) Oh, I could not think of leaving you. By Jove, here's a bullfinch and no gate!

MODERNA, excitedly.

A bullfinch, on a gate? Oh, show me. I do so love them. I've a cage of them at home.

CAPTAIN PROVIS.

I mean this hawthorn hedge. . . . (Aside, as MODERNA scrambles through the hedge minus her hat, and with several scratches.) One would think it was her first day out; yet Mrs. D. told me? . . . (Aloud.) Lost your hat? I'll fetch it. . . . By Jove, what hair!

MODERNA.

Oh, thank you. I am afraid I am a dreadful drag on you?

CAPTAIN PROVIS, gallantly.

Not at all. Enjoying myself awfully! . . . Hallo, what's happened? . . . Hang it all, the brute has gone down a drain.

MODERNA, joyfully.

Then he's safe.   I'm *so* glad !

CAPTAIN PROVIS, aside.

How refreshing a little sentiment is nowadays !   (Aloud.)
I'm afraid not ; we shall soon dig him out.

MODERNA.

What !   *Dig* him out ?

CAPTAIN PROVIS.

Certainly ; hounds deserve blood.

MODERNA, shuddering.

How disgusting !   And will you really kill him ?

CAPTAIN PROVIS.

Rather !   You mustn't be so tender-hearted—spoil all
your fun. . . . (Looking at his watch.)   Clinking run, that !
Thirty-five minutes without a check. . . . We shall try
Bagley covert now, you will see.

Hounds are put in and there is a long wait.

CAPTAIN PROVIS.

I'm afraid, after all, it's going to prove a blank.

MODERNA.

A blank !   What's that ?

CAPTAIN PROVIS.

No fox in it.

MODERNA.

How stupid—like the "history" of Viola in "Twelfth Night." (Mr. Provis stares.) Oh, listen, there's a poor dog whining! He must be hurt.

CAPTAIN PROVIS.

Hurt! Not he, he's got on to a fox.

MODERNA, shuddering.

Don't speak of it !

CAPTAIN PROVIS, aside.

She does look ripping . . . but . . . (Aloud.) How long do you stay here, Miss Maskelyne?

MODERNA, laughing.

Two days — three days — as long as I am amused.

CAPTAIN PROVIS.

As long as you and Mrs. Deverel can hit it off together, eh? Two pretty women in a house—! There is a fellow called Coniston up there now, I'm told, always sets all the women by the ears. . . . (Aside.) By Jove, she looks lovely when she blushes! (Aloud.) I hope to call when you are there, Miss Maskelyne . . . you must have seen how very much I . . .

MODERNA.

Oh, please take care !

CAPTAIN PROVIS.

What's the matter ?

MODERNA.

I thought your horse was going to kick mine.

CAPTAIN PROVIS.

No fear! But he's a good "peddy" horse, I can tell you.

MODERNA.

"Peddy"! Is that a hunting word for pretty?

CAPTAIN PROVIS.

No, no! a horse with a pedigree, don't you know? Don't let us talk of hunting. . . . I want to ask you . . .

MODERNA.

Listen, wasn't· that the horn?

CAPTAIN PROVIS.

To ask you . . .

MODERNA.

Look, everybody is going! Something must be happening.

CAPTAIN PROVIS.

They've found! Confound it all!

The field moves on.

CAPTAIN PROVIS.

I hope your mare doesn't dislike water?

MODERNA.

Not when she is thirsty, I suppose. Why?

CAPTAIN PROVIS, laughing in a superior manner.

Only there is a stiffish water jump coming,—Hendon brook. However, it may be more amiable than last week.

MODERNA.

Amiable? Oh, Selima is very amiable, don't you think?

CAPTAIN PROVIS.

Like her rider. But I meant—it's a way we have of putting it—the Hendon brook, you know, sometimes it is a brimmer with rotten banks. Then you mightn't get on with it. Here it comes! Hold up! Don't haul at her mouth like that! Heavens! What a shave! (MODERNA barely manages to land on the other side, hugging her mare's neck.)

CAPTAIN PROVIS.

Halloa; there's young Heaviside turned a spread eagle into the next field.

MODERNA, looking up into the sky.

An eagle! Oh, how curious! You must write to the *Field.*

CAPTAIN PROVIS, aside.

Good Lord, she is too great a donkey for anything. (Aloud.) What are you hanging back for?

MODERNA, fumbling with her hat.

Stop! my hair is coming down!

CAPTAIN PROVIS.

Mustn't stop—hounds are too full of running. (Aside.)

Why can't she keep her hair up like other people? (Aloud.) Look out for those rails! (Aside.) Funked it, by Jove! (Aloud.) Get to one side, quick! Gad! that was a near thing!

MODERNA, innocently.

What was the matter?

CAPTAIN PROVIS, gravely.

You must never stop short at timber like that. You forget that there was the whole field behind you.

MODERNA.

But there was another field in front. How silly you are!

CAPTAIN PROVIS.

I mean riders. You would have been crushed in a moment. No one could pull their horses in at that pace!

MODERNA.

It reminds me of the last part of "The Gadsbys," . . . Kipling, you know. All right, I'll remember.

CAPTAIN PROVIS, aside.

Hang her literary allusions. (Aloud.) Come on, I'll look after you. Take care of the next fence, it is rather a stretcher. (Aside.) She simply can't ride a damn. (MODERNA evades the "stretcher" and finds a gap lower down.)

CAPTAIN PROVIS, aside.

Never knew that mare refuse before! (Shouting.) Keep back! keep back! Good heavens! she's ridden over a hound!

MODERNA, calling back.

Oh, I've dropped my hat, Captain Provis!

CAPTAIN PROVIS.

No, by Jove, this is too much! I wash my hands of her. (Pretends not to hear and rides on. MODERNA pulls up to laugh as Mrs. DEVEREL, Lord CONISTON, and BILLY DANVERS come up.)

MRS. FRED DEVEREL.

What *are* you laughing at, Moderna? and what a mess you are in—all mud and scratches!

MODERNA.

I know,—but I've had such a good time!

MRS. FRED DEVEREL.

You don't look as if you had. . . . Captain Provis doesn't seem to have taken very good care of you. . . . (Aside.) Has it . . . has he . . .?

MODERNA.

Why, oh why did you tell him I could ride?

BILLY DANVERS.

Well, you *can* ride, just!

MODERNA.

I have nearly spoilt my day proving to Captain Provis that I can't. Tell Lord Coniston what you said to me, Flossie—I'm sorry I can't concur with you both in your plans for me. . . . Look here, Billy, we mustn't stop.

Stick to me and we will soon catch them up. Come along and watch me break my neck. (Flicking her mare.) Poor old Selima! I've been giving you away! (Rides on.)

CONISTON.

She'll kill herself! She's so reckless.

MRS. FRED DEVEREL.

Nonsense. You don't understand women. That is only pose. Something—or somebody—has put her out!

XXVIII

AFTER dinner. Lord CONISTON and MODERNA in the Hall. It is ten o'clock.

MODERNA.

Good-night, Edward.

CONISTON.

Good-night. Why are you going so early?

MODERNA, wearily.

'Don't know. 'Got a headache. At least I said so.

CONISTON, coldly·

You must be tired after all that—?

MODERNA.

You disapprove of me, I suppose?

CONISTON.

Perhaps you disapprove of yourself?

MODERNA, airily.

No!

CONISTON.

Why should you? You do Miss Letty Lind much credit, I am sure.

MODERNA, pettishly.

I'm sure I didn't want to dance—but Flossie was so positive—and one hates refusing—

CONISTON.

Why should you refuse? What is the good of learning if one doesn't mean to perform? You can't dance under a bushel. Poor little Violet Fleming would have given her eyes to be able to do likewise.

MODERNA.

Her mother would not let her. . . . That isn't her pose at all! . . . But Flossie really gave me no peace when once she found I could dance.

CONISTON.

Mrs. Deverel wants to make it go, naturally; and we men are so sleepy and stupid after a day's hunting—

MODERNA, interrupting.

Oh, I say, I never supposed that horrid little Provis was a friend of the family! . . . Some one is sure to tell him to-night that I am not the duffer I pretended to be.

CONISTON, laughing.

Your faithful Billy will be sure to chaff him about it.

MODERNA, abruptly.

Edward, will you do something for me?

CONISTON.

Anything—in reason.

MODERNA.

It isn't in reason.

CONISTON.

Out of reason, then.

MODERNA.

Ah, now you are nice. I am glad you came here, though I'll own I was dreadfully vexed at first to find that you had accepted the Deverels' invitation.

CONISTON.

Why?

MODERNA.

Because I was cross with you; you scolded me so the last time you saw me in London, and made me do a dreadfully rude thing. Poor Ned Tremaine; it was not his fault—the woman tempted him (laughing)—but I have never been able to bring myself to speak to him since!

CONISTON.

Did I scold you? I had no right to scold you.

MODERNA.

No, for you are not responsible for me . . . so . . . will you do what I ask you now? Will you take me into the smoking-room to-night, and hide me there, so that I can hear what they say?

CONISTON, quickly.

Oh, I couldn't do that.

MODERNA.

Yes, you could; there's a curtain.

CONISTON.

I meant morally couldn't.

MODERNA.

You said just now that you had nothing to do with my morals . . . oh, Edward, do be nice—you might! I must—I must hear Provis on the " Belle's Stratagem ! "

CONISTON.

You might hear a good deal about it. It wasn't very good form—excuse me !—was it?

MODERNA.

I daresay not; but you don't know how Flossie vexed me ! Never mind that . . . Edward, I have always wanted so much to hear how men talk. A woman's intellect is so maimed and stunted by her enforced ignorance and narrowness. She hasn't a chance, she goes about with moral blinkers on—she can't see all round—

CONISTON.

No, thank the Lord !

MODERNA.

It would be like seeing the other side of the moon.

CONISTON.

The moon isn't so silly as to show it. (Shaking his head.)
You wouldn't like it—indeed—you would be miserable.

MODERNA.

I can stand a good deal, I assure you.   I am not thin-
skinned.   It will be delightful to hear the truth for once.
You must make them talk of me. . . .

CONISTON.

Don't, dear, please.

MODERNA.

Don't you see, Edward, I may never have a chance
again—I am supposed to have gone to bed with a
headache.   I'll only do it this once . . . I promise . . . it
is only because I want to know . . . it would be good for
me, it would teach me wisdom . . .

CONISTON, laughing.

Oh no, nothing would do that.

MODERNA.

Well, anyhow, do manage it for me.

CONISTON.

Don't, dear.

MODERNA, angrily.

Edward, you make me tired with your "don't, dears."
I mean to do it, so there! whether you help me or not.
Do you remember Shakespeare?—"And if she will she
will, you may depend on't;"—

CONISTON.

"And when she won't she won't, and there's an end
on't." Let it be won't, dear, and an end of it, I beg
you. It is a hateful thing you are asking me to do.

MODERNA.

What are you afraid of? What would happen?

CONISTON.

Men are such brutes!

MODERNA.

You say dreadfully clever, sarcastic things, I suppose?

CONISTON.

On the contrary! We say intensely stupid things. You
wouldn't believe it, how awfully dull we are!

MODERNA.

I thought you meant you would talk such horrors, I
should come from behind that curtain with gray hair. . . .
Well, Edward, I don't mean to argue. Will you help
me or not? I mean to do it; but I am less likely to

be found out if you hide me, as you know where they all sit. (She moves towards the billiard room.) Are you coming?

CONISTON, slowly following her.

Yes . . . like an idiot !

MODERNA, sweetly.

I see you have some little regard for me. (They enter the billiard room. She goes behind a curtain.) Take care my foot does not show. Oh, isn't it stuffy.! This heavy rep curtain will make my cheeks so hot. . . .

CONISTON.

If it were only the curtain—! Moderna, give it up! Come out! . . . No, you can't now—keep quiet, here they come! (Aside.) I wish I were through this.

Enter FRED DEVEREL the host, ARTHUR DEVEREL, BILLY DANVERS, Captains PROVIS, HEAVISIDE, and Sir HENRY GRAHAM. FRED DEVEREL and Sir HENRY GRAHAM play billiards. The others smoke.

SIR HENRY.

Did you have much to do, Prov.? I take it I didn't lose much, did I?

CAPTAIN PROVIS.

No, but *I* did. It was a fairish run, but they spoilt it for me—gave me that dancing-girl,—what's her name?

BILLY DANVERS.

Oh, come, Prov., you know you were awfully gone on her at the last Hunt Ball.

CAPTAIN PROVIS.

Was I? That's six months ago. Besides, that dancing to-night finished me. I must say I think it's bad form for society girls to try to cut out the professionals—they think there's nothing in it but showing their legs.

CONISTON.

Oh, come, Captain Provis—I am sure—

CAPTAIN PROVIS.

Well, that's just about all they can do. They are about as graceful as a kangaroo with the rheumatism. Just compare that girl—what's her infernal name?—with little Kitty Clayton, or even Maggie Brace! She's simply a duffer at it.

BILLY DANVERS.

What makes you so shirty about her, Provis?

CAPTAIN PROVIS.

You'd be shirty, Billy, if you'd had the best run since the frost spoilt for you by that beastly girl. She is as big a duffer on a horse as on a floor.

CONISTON and DANVERS.

Ha! Ha! Ha!

CAPTAIN PROVIS.

Yes, you may well laugh; but it was worse than you think. (Looking round curiously.) Why, Billy, what the devil are you laughing at? Don't be a donkey—don't make an infernal laughing jackass of yourself! Why, Coniston, are you taken bad too? What is it?

S

BILLY DANVERS, laughing unrestrainedly.

You owl! you idiot! you infernal donkey! Don't you know that . . .

CONISTON.

Why, Captain Provis, did you never hear?

CAPTAIN PROVIS.

What? What?

BILLY DANVERS.

Only that Miss Maskelyne, the girl *we* call Moderna, because she's more in the know, and more in the go than—anybody—

CAPTAIN PROVIS.

Well—what don't I know?

CONISTON, still laughing.

Why, that Miss Maskelyne is simply the best rider to hounds in the whole county.

BILLY DANVERS.

The straightest goer you'll find anywhere. Where were you raised not to know that, old man?

SIR HENRY, chalking his cue.

Ha, ha! Prov., you've been got at this time! I wonder at you. Yes, she's straight enough over a fence, whatever she is in a drawing-room!

CONISTON.

Come, you know, Graham—

SIR HENRY, aiming.

Oh, no particular harm.—If you like that sort of girl,
that's the sort of girl you'd like—I don't.

CONISTON, angrily.

You don't, don't you?

SIR HENRY, making his stroke.

No, I don't. I don't care much for a lead from a
woman when I'm riding to hounds; but, hang it, I
say, I won't stand having the running made for me by
a girl at a dance or a dinner. Bad form! Deuced
bad form!

CONISTON, getting up.

Confound it all! I—

HEAVISIDE.

Don't you defend her, Con. It's just what I think too.
That girl's all over the place. I remember her at her
sister's wedding. She thinks every man she talks to is
gone on her; and she's always trying to persuade a
fellow she's gone on him. I don't like it myself—it's
sickening! Look at Miss Fleming now—nice, quiet—

BILLY DANVERS.

Dull, I think. Well, I won't say much for Moderna's
manners—I won't say much for Moderna's morals, if it
comes to that—but she's very good fun, and her riding
is A1.

CONISTON.

You shut up, Billy!

BILLY DANVERS, innocently.

Well, she does ride straight, Coniston, doesn't she ?
Why, Provis, couldn't you see how she sat her horse ?

CAPTAIN PROVIS.

All hunched up whenever I looked, like a blessed old
farmer's wife going to market.

BILLY DANVERS, sniggering.

Now, I wonder what Moderna was humbugging you for ?

CAPTAIN PROVIS.

Humbugging me ?   Impossible !

BILLY DANVERS.

Well, it seems she didn't find it impossible.   Ha ! ha !

CAPTAIN PROVIS, thoughtfully.

By God, if I thought that—I'd—

CONISTON, sternly.

What would you do, Captain Provis ?

CAPTAIN PROVIS, very angry.

Never mind.   I know something ; and if that girl tries
any of her damned tricks on me, I'll show her up !

THE HOST.

Let the girl alone, can't you, Provis ?   She may be a bit
fast and a trifle foolish, but . . .

CONISTON.

Captain Provis ! I must trouble you to remember that Miss Maskelyne is a connection of mine. . . .

CAPTAIN PROVIS.

By Jove, I didn't know. I'm sure I beg your pardon.

BILLY DANVERS, to Coniston.

Don't get your shirt out, old man !

CONISTON.

Shut up, Billy, you damned young idiot. I don't want your apologies, Captain Provis ; and I'll just trouble you to leave Miss Maskelyne alone for the future.

CAPTAIN PROVIS.

Certainly I will. Never would, you know, if I had known she was a connection of yours. (To his host.) Hang it, my weed's out. No thank you, I don't think I'll light another. Turn in, I think. Rather tired. Lots of pottering about that last woodland. In and out of it all day, and couldn't get hold of my second horse. Tired horse tires a man awfully. Good-night.

Exit yawning. Others at intervals follow. CONISTON stays. MODERNA comes slowly from behind the curtain. She puts her hands before her face, and tries to pass him.

CONISTON.

I am so sorry, dear.

MODERNA.

Sorry ! What's the good of being sorry now ? You exposed me to it. Let me pass, please.

CONISTON.

Well, of all the unfair—

MODERNA.

Yes, I am unfair as well as all the other things.   Let me
go !   I never wish to see *any* of you again.   (Sobbing.)   I
never thought men were such brutes !

CONISTON.

We are ; we are !

MODERNA.

Oh, don't include yourself, please !   You came out of it
all right.   You see you had the advantage of the others.
You happened to know there was a woman hidden in
the room.

CONISTON, fiercely.

Do you mean to say that you think I should have
spoken differently if you had not been there ?

MODERNA, petulantly.

Oh, how do I know?   It all sounded very fine and
high-flown.   I believe you got it up so that you might
appear . . .   Let me go, I don't know what I am
saying !

CONISTON.

You saw I quarrelled with all my friends ?

MODERNA.

Your friends !   Do you call those wretches your friends ?

CONISTON.

They were your friends too till now—and yet they were always like that. Don't be unjust, Moderna, it is the average man. They speak as they find; they take their rough, coarse view of life; they don't pretend to go into matters deeply—they are not subtle. If a girl says or does so and so, they assess her at a certain valuation. A woman can't be too careful.

MODERNA.

No, not in a world of howling wild beasts, ready to misinterpret every speech, every action! . . . Oh, it maddens me to think of it! . . . One laughs and talks in one's silly innocence, and they listen complacently and lead one on; and all the while they are inferring the worst . . .

CONISTON.

Yes, they do; it's a way they have.

MODERNA, violently.

Are you not ashamed of them?

CONISTON.

One can't undertake to be ashamed of the whole of human kind . . . And Provis was a little bitter against you for that trick you played him to-day.

MODERNA.

Sir Henry Graham—and Captain Heaviside—whom I have always be so kind to—

CONISTON.

Too kind, I am afraid!

MODERNA.

They are so plain, and so dull! The other women neglect them so . . . I tried . . .

CONISTON.

The meanest man thinks he is more than a match for the nicest woman in the world.

MODERNA.

I know one thing, I'll never shake hands with any of them again!

CONISTON.

You must. You must not let then notice anything. It would be dreadful! Go to bed now like a good girl, and go to sleep and forget it all!

MODERNA.

How can I go to sleep? How can I meet them all to-morrow, as if I hadn't seen their hateful natures all spread out before me?

CONISTON.

You've done it up till now.

MODERNA.

Yes, but then I didn't know. How can I sit down to breakfast with a man who thinks I am in love with him?

CONISTON.

Good heavens ! do you think it would be the first time ?
Men are so vain.   You can bear it when it's the other
way round, too.

MODERNA.

It doesn't disgrace a man to be in love.

CONISTON.

And do you think it is a disgrace to a woman ?

MODERNA.

We cannot stay up here alone all night arguing abstract
questions. . . .

CONISTON.

No, by Jove.   I don't know what I am thinking of to
let you stay.   Go to bed, will you ?

MODERNA.

Yes. . . . (Moves into the corridor.) . . . You've been very kind
to me, Edward . . . I don't know why I was so cross to
you.   I beg your pardon.   It was all my fault . . . my
self-will. . . .   Will you do something for me ?

CONISTON.

What ?   Call Sir Henry out ?   Call 'em all out ?   (Laughing.)
I should get a dozen challenges to-morrow myself, if
duelling was in fashion.

MODERNA.

Yes, you gave it them pretty strong. . . .   No, it is

.

this.   I want you to meet me at the East Gate—in half
an hour—

CONISTON flatly.

I won't!   Enough folly for one night.

MODERNA, earnestly.

Yes, Edward, the East Gate, in half an hour . . .
sh—sh—don't ask questions . . . do it . . . do it . . . I
beg of you, dear Edward . . . please, please . . . you must
help me . . . I shall drown myself if you don't.

CONISTON, hoarsely.

Nonsense! . . .   Stop, Moderna, I can't let you beg me
like this . . . I'll go there . . . but if you don't come I'll
conclude you have gone to bed like a sensible girl. . . .
You will think better of it, won't you?   It isn't so serious
as you think.

MODERNA, beginning to go upstairs.

Oh, I didn't think Billy Danvers would turn against me!
My own Billy, that I have brought up from a child . . .

CONISTON.

Don't cry over Billy.   He's not worth it.   No heart!
Good-night.   Sleep well . . . and forget . . .

MODERNA, on the top of the stairs.

Don't *you* forget.   (Meaningly.)   *Au revoir!*

XXIX

THE stable yard at Bleahope. A dogcart drawn out. MODERNA
with a lantern, manipulating the harness. Lord CONISTON comes up
behind her.

CONISTON.

Moderna !

MODERNA, handing him a strap.

Here, do this ! I quite forget how it goes.

CONISTON.

What *does* this mean ?

MODERNA.

Quick . . . help me . . . don't talk. Harness Kitty.
I am going to catch the mail for the south at Bellingham
Junction, and you are to come to the station with me,
and drive the pony back and put her in again.

CONISTON.

Where are you going ?

MODERNA, wildly.

Away . . . somewhere ! I won't shake hands with these
men again !

CONISTON.

What utter nonsense !

MODERNA.

May be, but I am going.

CONISTON.

But your people are all away on the Riviera.   You can't go home to an empty house.

MODERNA.

I'm going to Dolly's.   I live with her now.   I shall arrive at about breakfast-time.   I shall wire to her from Old Fort.   Oh, Edward, don't argue!   I can put the pony in without your help, of course . . . but be kind, and help me.   It's all right, I've left the traditional note on my pin-cushion for Flossie . . . she knows I'm quite mad!

CONISTON.

I really think you are.   Did any one ever— ?

MODERNA.

I daresay no one ever did, but I do.   Some one wrote my epitaph once—"She was made for irregular situations.' . . . Quiet, Kitty!

CONISTON.

Moderna, you mustn't go.   I won't let you.   Wait till morning.

MODERNA.

Then I couldn't get away till the afternoon.   (Appealingly.) Edward, you are the only friend I have!   I assure you I can pull it through, if you will help me?

CONISTON, leading out the pony.

Do you remember what you said just now?

MODERNA.

No, what ? I said a number of things in haste I shall repent at leisure, no doubt.

CONISTON.

That I shouldn't have stood up for you if I hadn't known you were hidden behind the curtain ?

MODERNA, wearily, getting up into the cart.

Oh, yes, I daresay you would have defended me, out of contrariety—you drive, will you ?—for you know, in your heart of hearts, you agreed with them ?

CONISTON.

I agree with Provis ! Good heavens ! No !

MODERNA.

Not in the manner, but in the substance. You know you think I . . . you know you do disapprove of me ?

CONISTON.

I think, if you ask me, you have some very bad friends.

MODERNA.

I don't see why you should put it on my friends. One makes oneself; one is responsible for oneself. I was born, I developed according to the laws of my growth, like an oak from an acorn. No one interfered. I should like to have seen them interfere. I always did exactly as I liked.

CONISTON.

I know.   Your mother—

MODERNA.

You are not to say a word against her.   How could she help it?   I "growed," like Topsy, and I growed bad.

CONISTON.

Don't abuse yourself.   I won't have it.

MODERNA.

Edward, be serious.

CONISTON, laughing.

I am serious.   I won't allow anybody to abuse you, not even yourself.

MODERNA.

Ah, but you must not abuse my friends.

CONISTON.

Your ideals, then.

MODERNA.

What are they?   I think I have none.

CONISTON.

Then I should advise you to find some.   A woman without ideals is an uncomfortable, inhuman, unnatural creature, to my thinking.

MODERNA.

A woman without conventional ideals is surely a finer,

nobler, freer creature than the wretched Helot of custom . . .

CONISTON, delicately whipping up the pony.

There you go ! . . . I begin to think that conventions are useful—picturesque even. They put a kind of atmosphere round a woman—a sort of softening haze, delightfully unreal, I daresay . . .

MODERNA.

Something for a man to destroy when he marries her ! Men always choose a woman with conventions, it seems to me. Violet Fleming, for instance ? She has little nets to keep her front hair in order, and a microscopic little prayer-book to take to Church, and a set of little principles to regulate her conduct. She is full of little methodical habits that would grow into fads if she were an old maid. Marrying her would be like putting one's money into the Funds. Safe but slow.

CONISTON, thoughtfully.

Yes, a man might do worse than marry the retiring Violet. Some one will, I suppose.

MODERNA.

Some one ?

CONISTON, quickly.

Not me. Provis, perhaps ?

A Pause.

MODERNA, shyly.

I always thought, Edward, do you know, that you were going to marry that beautiful Mrs. Belinfante, whose portrait I saw in Mr. Tremaine's studio? . . .

CONISTON.

Did you? . . . Look here, do you mind having the seat put back a bit? Will you go to her head while I do it?

*   *   *   *   *

MODERNA, fondling the pony.

Sweet, nice Kitty! I love you. Is it done, Edward? (She gets in again. They start.) No, I don't think Violet Fleming would do for you. Do you remember proposing to me, once, when I was young and innocent like that?

CONISTON. ˙

I do ; and you refused me so politely, so seriously—not chaffingly, as you would now.

MODERNA.

I always refused even an invitation to dance very solemnly in those days. I was an awful baby. And did you never wonder who your rival was?

CONISTON.

Yes, often. I used to scrutinise all your mother's guests with that view . . . I believe I finally fixed on Gontram Vere—only he seemed such an ass?

MODERNA.

Was! And he never even asked me.

CONISTON.

People said he did. . . . But, Moderna, since we are in the vein of confidences, would you mind telling me who the man really was ?

MODERNA.

An actor. A man I had never even spoken to.

CONISTON.

But how, then . . .

MODERNA.

Stage-fever. Lots of girls had it then—and for Calder-Marston. Cecilia Riddell got quite thin over it, till she went to Girton. You have no idea how wild we all were over that man.

CONISTON.

And you only saw him across the foot-lights ! What odd things girls are ! Why, if you had seen him come drunk into the " Savage " every night of his life, and abuse his wife to the fellows there, you would soon have been disillusioned. And it was for the sake of a man you had never spoken to, that you . . .

MODERNA.

Don't you see ? We fell in love with " Hamlet " or " Iago "—yes, we even loved him as Iago,—not the man Marston. . . . Look at the lash of the whip ! . . . it is like a fiery white snake writhing in the light of the lantern. We wanted the lantern . . . there is no moon . . . and you drive so fast . . .

CONISTON, laughing.

I thought you always preferred to "take things fast." Are you afraid ?

T

MODERNA.

Of your spilling me ? . . . No. (Peering into the night.) I believe I can see the signal at Bellingham.

CONISTON, quickly.

It's not down ?

MODERNA.

Oh no . . . heaps of time. . . . What were we talking about ?   That was a lucky escape you had, wasn't it ?

CONISTON.

What ?   I assure you, I shan't let her down.

MODERNA.

I wasn't thinking of the pony.   I meant (bitterly) an escape of marrying a girl who is "damned bad form "—and "all over the place "—whose manners and morals even Billy Danvers won't defend. . . .

CONISTON.

Don't quote those idiots, please.

MODERNA.

But it's quite true !   I wouldn't marry *me* if I were a man.   I think I should plague my husband's life out, should I not ?

CONISTON.

I verily believe you would—if he didn't love you !

MODERNA.

Even if he did !—worse if he did !   But there's no

chance of that. I'm not the kind of girl a man falls in love with, now, or would want to be married to. I don't try to be. I'm not a fair Circassian, bred and brought up for the noble profession of marriage. I don't live up to that ideal. I have arranged my life quite differently.

CONISTON, drily.

So I see.

A Silence.

.   MODERNA.

Oh, I do wish we were there !

CONISTON.

Why ?   Are you so dreadfully uncomfortable ?

MODERNA.

Dreadfully.

CONISTON.

Can't we arrange the cushions for you—or something ?

MODERNA, twisting about.

No, it isn't that. I don't want anything altered. I am not comfortable . . . in my mind. (Violently.) I don't see why I should be made to feel so small. I have done nothing wrong.

CONISTON.

Nothing wrong, of course.

MODERNA.

But I feel as if I had . . . all wrong, and ashamed, snubbed, and apologetic. I feel as if I were quite alone somehow. You seem to sit there and turn a cold brown frieze shoulder to me. . . .

CONISTON, kindly.

I can't help it's being brown frieze, dear ; but it isn't cold, and I can't drive properly in the dark and turn round to you as well. What are we to do ?

MODERNA.

Nothing, only don't express so much moral condemnation with your back. You can't think how it oppresses me ! I could cry. . . .

CONISTON.

Don't, for heaven's sake !

MODERNA.

Let *me* drive, then ?

CONISTON.

Then we would miss the train. Be quiet, dear, and don't imagine things. I am not reproving you. I haven't the right . . . or the wish. . . .

MODERNA.

But I want us to be friends.

CONISTON.

So we are, always, only (laughing) don't expect me to follow in the wild paths where your theories are going to lead you. I am what is called a plain man ; and, frankly, I don't take to them.

MODERNA.

You a plain man ?

CONISTON.

I mean old-fashioned in ideas. I have seen the world
—a good deal of it—and I have a great deal more respect
for women than most of the men I know who have got
their illusions rubbed off. And I have never seen any
good come of the modern spirit of dissatisfied curiosity
and restlessness in women, who want to be different to
other women—who can't conform to what the wisdom
of ages has decreed for them. It's bad form, to say the
least of it.

MODERNA.

I know you think it "not nice." It isn't "nice" or
dignified for a woman to assert herself. But somebody
must. Edward, you are very narrow !

CONISTON.

Yes, I begin to glory in it.

MODERNA.

And you don't understand women one little bit.

CONISTON.

I understand you, I think. . . . Oh, it seems to me such
pity . . .

MODERNA.

What's a pity ?

CONISTON.

Nothing, nothing, I beg your pardon. Don't let us
discuss this. See if you can make out the signal ?

278

MODERNA.

It's down ! The train is signalled ! It was before !
How we have dawdled !

CONISTON.

All right, you shan't miss it. . . . Here we are ! Steady,
mare ! I'll take your ticket. Here, boy, hold her a
moment. (They go into the station. He looks round.) Not a soul
to go by this train. Shall *I* go with you, Moderna ? I
didn't offer before, for fear of compromising you, but I
don't like your going that long way alone.

MODERNA, getting into a compartment.

And who would take the trap back ? It's all right, I'm
not afraid. (Shivering.) How cold it is !

CONISTON.

Poor little thing ! You look so small and thin, and
your little chin so sharp. Let me come with you !

MODERNA.

No, thank you. But come and see me when you come
back to town, will you ?

CONISTON.

Where ?

MODERNA.

At Dolly Tremaine's.

CONISTON, stiffly.

Are you going there ? No—I don't think I can call on
you at Miss Tremaine's. I'll wait till you are home in
Queen's Gate again. . . .

MODERNA

Oh, if you wait till then!... I see I must do without you. Good-bye, we are just off.

CONISTON, raising his cap.

Do without me? If I can help you in any way?..

MODERNA, as the train moves on.

You can't. Besides you have just refused. Good-night!

XXX

A Christmas Party at the FLEMINGS'. MODERNA is sitting apart by herself.

MODERNA

I wish I was dead

I am twenty-seven years old. I really never noticed it till now. I am perfectly sound in wind and limb, as they say of horses; I can't find a wrinkle on my face if I look ever so hard; I could dance all night without stopping . . . but no matter . . . I have had my day, and the sooner I realise the fact the better.

Oh dear, what a long day it has been, now I look back on it! I've done everything. I've done all the things girls do, and a good many things girls *don't* do. I've scribbled, and daubed, and strummed, and acted, and tried everything under the sun. And now I'm living with a little lady-journalist, in rooms over a shop in the Strand, and I've quarrelled with my people about her, and they have gone abroad, and I'm here, alone, in London.   Alone, for Dolly hardly counts, she is out nearly all day.   I'm quite independent—quite!

It's Christmas Eve.   I don't go in for being senti-mental about Christmas, but it seems odd to be alone, somehow, at this time.   I believe I could almost get up a kind of Christmas feeling.   But not with Dolly.   Oh, I am sick of her!   I had rather be with them in the Riviera, and that's saying a good deal.

But it is my own wish, so I ought not to complain ; I like my own way, and I have got it.   I always have, all my life.   I ought to be content.

I've had a good time, on the whole.   I came out, and was made a fuss of, and lots of people fell in love with me—and that's always supposed to be pleasant. Not for them, poor things! . . . but then, no woman ever thinks of that—till after!

I've danced and flirted and gossiped and amused myself generally, and made a business of pleasure.   If all the dancing shoes I've worn out were collected, what a heap there would be !   And all the frocks I have worn, and torn, and put my foot through—and the bouquets I've ruined—and the compliments I've had—and the offers I've refused . . . Oh yes, I was a success, not a doubt of it !

And now, what is the good of it all ?   I have made a certain number of people quite miserable, but I've never been in love myself—not once—at least I think not.

I've been told, times out of number, that I have "no

heart." Men always say that when they are refused, to
save their own vanity. I wonder if it is true in my case?
No one cares now whether I have a heart or not.
It's all different. I have got a certain number of friends
whose step suits mine, who ask me for dances—but
without enthusiasm—and have the want of tact to talk
to me of this or that "dear little thing over there, who
is enjoying herself so"! They say I'm a "good sort"
and "a real friend." A friend! What has friendship
to do in a ball-room?

At any rate, it doesn't exist between girls. They
don't want to be bothered with other girls in a ball-room.
What can you do for each other if you are friends?
Own she's pretty if you are asked—not defeat her little
plans if you know them—tell her when her hair is
coming down—and tuck in her dress-lace when it shows
—and introduce her to your cast-off partners? I've
often done that. Violet Fleming will do it for me in a
moment if I catch her eye. I won't. I don't want
charity dances. I should say I was engaged. I will
not dance with veterans, or boys. I had rather sit out.

How dreadfully melancholy dance music is! I never
noticed it so much before. I could lie down on the
floor this very minute and howl, if I were to let myself
go. It is as if they were all dancing on a grave.

Suppose I were to cross the room and talk to Mrs.
Fleming, and ask her if she means to have influenza
again this winter? Anything to seem occupied! No,
I see she is asleep; and if she was not, she would only
tell me of Violet's perfections. I see them . . . everybody sees them . . . oh dear!

There *is* Violet with Edward. He is looking at her exactly as he used to look at me, years ago, before I forfeited his respect. Yes, I have forfeited his respect. I live with Dolly, whom he doesn't think nice. I don't either, but I can't own it. He has never been to see me since that wild flight of mine from Bleahope a month ago. I wonder if he took the trap back all right? I have never heard since from the Deverels. I suppose Flossie was cross . . . I sometimes thought she was a little jealous of me and Edward. . . .

Poor Edward . . . he looks grave . . . I daresay he hates meeting me? We have to meet, of course, but somehow, I fancy he takes every opportunity of not dancing with me—waits till I am engaged, or going, or something, so that it never comes off. If he were to really come and talk to me I should think the end of the world had come. I had much rather he didn't. We don't get on somehow, now. We should only feel awkward.

However, I needn't be afraid of his coming to me. I am much too horrid.

I should not be surprised if he got engaged to Violet Fleming. She is delightfully young, and naïve, and enthusiastic. I know he thinks so. She has the reddest arms I ever saw.

Oh, don't let me be spiteful !

I know that cadence. The valse is nearly over. They will all come by. That's the most awful moment of all. I wish I was talking to some one. It is so hateful to try and look unconcerned, and as if I were sitting here because I liked it.

Oh, I can't bear it. I'll marry. I'll marry Mr.
Brown. He adores me. He pretends he isn't a bit
shocked at my Bohemianism. He would even tolerate
Dolly for my sake. Well, it's more than I can do
sometimes. I shall condescend to let him see that I
don't absolutely dislike him. I shall be a clergyman's
wife. How terrible! But it is the only way out of it
. . . for me!

Yes, for me, but for him? I don't love him. How
could I? I should have to tell him; and even a Mr.
Brown is not so abject as to want to marry a woman
who tells him point blank that she can only promise to
tolerate him. And if I don't tell him it would be mean.

No, I'll go into a convent. How dull! Not so dull
though, as marrying Mr. Brown.

I wish my people would come home. I would go
back and do the prodigal daughter, and beg their pardon
for wanting to be independent, and ask them to let me
live with them again. That's dull, too, but less binding
than marriage. I shall be a bachelor-girl to the end of
the chapter.

Here they all come! I must try to look unconcerned.
I know every stick of my fan by heart. It has seen me
through many "situations," but I will pretend it interests
me deeply. And I can see over the top of it!

Here's the first couple! Billy Danvers with Miss
Forrest. I was Billy's first love, and he is trying hard to
make Grace Forrest think *she* is. Let him!

Mrs. Jenkyn and our host! She's a widow. How
jealous Verona and I used to be of her! We used to
study her little ways. She was a widow then, and she's

a widow now—prefers it. I wish some one would make me a widow! What *am* I saying? But she's ten years older than I am, and she laughs like a child. That comes of being a widow.

Here's Arthur Deverel. He really was in love with me once, so now he detests me. "A man scorned" is much worse than a woman scorned. He won't even look at me. No . . . straight past!

Why, here's Violet—with Mr. Darcy. I thought she was sitting out in the blue room with Edward! And Edward!—alone!

May you see me home, Edward? Why . . . yes . . . if you like. In half an hour? Ten minutes? I'll go and put on my cloak.

Oh, good heavens! The end of the world—or the beginning?

XXXI

The Strand at midnight. Lord CONISTON *and* MODERNA *alight from a hansom. There is snow on the ground.*

MODERNA.

See, that is the Aerated bread shop on one side, and the spectacle shop on the other! This is our door. (Inserting her latch-key.) We are four flights up. Pity me! Good-night.

CONISTON.

May I not see you up?

MODERNA, jauntily.

Oh, I am not afraid, though we don't run to a single gas jet. (Opening the door on to a pitch-dark staircase.)

CONISTON.

I want to speak to you.

MODERNA.

Why did you not do it in the hansom, instead of discussing the weather and Violet Fleming? Very well, come along—but I warn you, Dolly is most likely sitting up doing her proofs. . . . Mind the step, and don't wake the Anarchist on the second floor.

CONISTON.

All right . . . (They progress slowly.) And who lives on this flight?

MODERNA.

Heart of Woman. It's a weekly. If it was light you would see a large placard on the door. I always feel it is quite indelicate to go any further . . . oh dear . . . (Pants.)

CONISTON.

Don't talk so much! You are quite out of breath. (MODERNA utters an exclamation.) Did you swear?

MODERNA, wearily.

No, I am not sunk quite so low as that! I put my foot through my flounce, that's all. Oh, will these stairs never end? I never found them so long before.

CONISTON.

You are tired, with dancing. . . .

MODERNA.

No—not with dancing. (Opens a door.) Here we are!
Why, it's quite dark ! Dolly has gone to bed and put
out the lamp . . .

CONISTON.

I had better go.

MODERNA.

Please don't leave me till I get a light. The room is
so full of shadows . . . I believe I am afraid . . . Help
me to find the matches. (Shivers.) It's all dark—and
cold—and wretched—

CONISTON.

And not *quite* dark. How odd it is ! I can see you
faintly, like a white, wandering ghost . . .

MODERNA.

Edward, if you talk of ghosts I shall scream out loud !
Gropes for matches.) They are generally here—in the
china dog. Where has that tiresome Dolly put . . .
Oh—h ! . . . What was that ?

CONISTON.

All right. The piano's open and I touched a note.

MODERNA.

Was that all ? What a fool I am ! I thought . . . oh,
Edward, do find the matches. I can't bear this a

moment longer. . . . There . . . I have knocked my head against that cornice. It hurts like anything . . . my head swims . . . where am I ? . . .

CONISTON.

In my arms, dear. Oh, won't you stay there ?

*   *   *   *   *

MODERNA, after a long pause.

And this is the end of me . . . ?

CONISTON.

Do you mind ?

MODERNA.

No, not so much as I thought . . . (Letting her head fall on his shoulder.) How soft this fur is ! Oh, Edward, I *am* so tired of it all—of Dolly, and Bohemia—and dances— and life, and literature, and everything ! You under- stand, I think.

CONISTON.

Yes, I do, I always did. That was my only merit. I understood you.

MODERNA.

I wasn't worth understanding. . . . Listen, here's Dolly. . .

DOLLY TREMAINE, putting her head in at the door.

Moderna ! is that you ? How late you are ! (Sees Conis- ton.) Oh ! . . .

Exit.

CONISTON.

What has she gone back for ?

MODERNA.

To put on a becoming tea-gown.   You must go before she comes back, I think.

CONISTON.

Very well.   And may I come to tea with you to-morrow?

MODERNA, significantly.

With me and Dolly?

CONISTON.

I can stand Miss Tremaine, I can stand anything—with you.

MODERNA.

I can hardly stand her myself, but you were not nice about her—confess?   (Pushing back her hair from her face.)   This is only a mood.   I am ashamed of it.   I shall be all right to-morrow.

CONISTON.

All right!—and all wrong for me?   Do you mean you will go back on me to-morrow?

MODERNA.

Are you happy, now, then?

CONISTON.

Yes.

MODERNA.

You are very good to me, dear . . . but this isn't the way a man would like it to happen . . . is it? . . . not picturesque . . . not romantic . . . a half-hysterical, nervous woman crying on your shoulder in the dark, because she's ill, and tired, and because she has been to a ball, and people haven't asked her to dance . . . and her vanity's hurt . . . a failure . . . a . . .

CONISTON, slowly.

Are you a failure ?   I never noticed.   You seem to me the nicest, sweetest, prettiest girl in London !

MODERNA.

Pretty !   I am glad it's dark, that you don't see my red eyes . . . What a fool I am !

CONISTON.

Be a fool, dear, an adorable fool !   I don't care what it is brings you to me, so long as you come.

MODERNA, rising and putting her hands on his shoulder.

Yes, I have come. . . . You know, Edward, you have not really asked me ?

CONISTON.

No man ought to propose to a woman twice.

MODERNA.

But . . .

CONISTON.

Yes, dear, I asked you once . . . you remember the first time ? . . . the second time, I   simply   take   you ! (Kisses her.)

THE END